Was it Love?

Was it Love?

NEHA SULTANIA

Srishti
PUBLISHERS & DISTRIBUTORS

Srishti Publishers & Distributors
Registered Office: N-16, C.R. Park
New Delhi – 110 019
Corporate Office: 212A, Peacock Lane
Shahpur Jat, New Delhi – 110 049
editorial@srishtipublishers.com

First published by
Srishti Publishers & Distributors in 2018

10 9 8 7 6 5 4 3 2 1

This is a work of fiction. The characters, places, organisations and events described in this book are either a work of the author's imagination or have been used fictitiously. Any resemblance to people, living or dead, places, events, communities or organisations is purely coincidental.

Printed and bound in India

Dear Vasudeva,

Who else can I dedicate my work to!

Only you have the power to bestow the gift of storytelling. You alone have carried me, scolded me, heard me, answered me and made me.

Acknowledgements

This piece of work, my debut novel, made me go through a plethora of emotions: good, bad and worst. From the days when I gave up to the days when I picked up again, and to this day, when this novel is complete and ready to embark its destined journey. There were days when a part of me believed it will never happen. My worst fear was if the story would ever make it out in the world from my laptop and land in the hand of a reader. But the dreams in my eyes would refuse to die. And whenever the flame of inspiration would flicker, these very important people would appear from time to time and whisper in my ear, "I am right here, don't you ever give up!"

This page of any book, thus, is the most important story behind a story. And as each story is woven through its protagonists, characters and antagonists, my story too has these dear friends and family who should be thanked here.

A myth who held the torch of guidance right through the beginning till the end, thanks for being the most difficult critic who I could never dodge.

My dear friend Meghna, who stood strong and forced me to send the manuscript to publishers. She carefully filtered out the impact of each rejection letter before it could ever reach to my conviction that this story is worth sharing with the world.

Vishal, you have been a great spouse throughout this journey, from sharing your beloved laptop with me to letting me freely express the story, however I wished to.

Mom and dad, I won't say thanks to you, because no words can ever justify your sacrifices in shaping up a difficult and stubborn child like me.

Very special thanks to Arup Bose and the entire team of Srishti Publishers for accepting my manuscript and putting their faith in my story. Firsts always hold a special place in our hearts, be it love or be it publishers.

There are some antagonists in my story, but I won't name them. As they say, "What's in the name?" But thanks to these special people, because without those betrayals and setbacks during the formative years of my life, I wouldn't have felt a deep wandering lust to explore my own existence and passion as a storyteller. You were the Ying to my Yang energy.

Lastly, but most importantly, heartfelt thanks to all the readers who will pick up the book and stick with me till the end.

I am made up of all the experiences brought by you people in my life.

Thank you!

The proposal

"Holy crap! Are we still alive, Leyla?" exclaimed Maya in shock and anger while Leyla took a sharp turn and parked the car outside Hotel 32nd Milestone in Gurgaon.

"Of course, we are! I don't drive that bad, darling." Leyla laughed as she stopped her white Toyota Corolla and hurriedly picked her Aldo bag from the back seat.

"When are you going to learn time management? I am fed up of risking my life with you!" Maya continued nagging while getting out of the car. "They will be so upset waiting for us, Leyla,"

"Oh c'mon Mayo! I don't know about your clock-watcher boyfriend Shahan, but Vikrant will give me a warm hug." Her giggles left Maya fuming. Leyla hugged her and said, "Sorry darling. This will be the last time that I have made you late." They rushed inside to attend Carnival Software Inc.'s annual event.

Leyla and Maya were best friends since school days. But somehow, as they grew up to chase their dreams, they lost touch after school. As luck would have it, both met again during an interview and ended up joining the same company. Vikrant was a senior software architect with Carnival Software Inc. A qualified software architect, Vikrant was a graduate from Princeton University. He was considered an asset by his employer, especially after acquiring project "Grey Pages", a professional website which he designed with his team in a very short time.

Shahan was leaving for California in a couple of weeks to pursue Executive MBA in finance. During last week's dinner at a fancy Chinese Restaurant in CP, Vikrant had invited them for his company's annual function at 32nd Milestone. Since Shahan also wanted quality time with Maya before leaving, he instantly accepted the invitation and suggested a stay over at Vikrant's house after the event.

Leyla was wearing a long georgette blue dress and had tied her hair into a bun. Her smooth skin, pale complexion and wide mouth made her fairly attractive. Big bright eyes studded her face, expressing the deepest emotion from the bottom of her heart. While they entered the hall, she quickly sighted Vikrant and Shahan among the other colleagues. It was always easy to notice Vikrant among the crowd because of his height. He was a big man.

Vikrant saw Leyla entering the room and came forward to receive her. He looked dapper in the cream colour T-shirt and brown cotton trousers. The metal black cap and brown leather shoes added to the sophistication. While hugging her tight, Vikrant murmured in Leyla's ears, "You look fab, my love!"

"So do you, Mr. Rao. God bless you!" whispered Leyla.

In his usual quirky tone, Vikrant smiled at Leyla and said, "Don't ask god to bless me. I am his opponent. May the higher devil bless me!" he snuggled Leyla and she snapped at him. "VICKY!!!" she said coyly while he held her tightly in his arms and laughed. Vikrant introduced the ladies to his colleagues. Leaving Maya with them, he took Leyla to introduce to his boss, Mr. Kamal Rana.

"Leyla, you are lucky to be with a man who is so talented and hardworking. Vikrant is a true leader. I like the way he handles his team. Sometimes I doubt whether he is a software engineer or a psychologist." Kamal chuckled looking at Leyla and she smiled with pride.

"I could be both! Don't get confused Kamal." Vikrant giggled in his witty style while sipping the sparkling scotch from his glass.

"Oh hold on, Vikrant! He definitely loves you a lot, Leyla. He has a picture of you hugging him as his desktop wallpaper," said Kamal. Vikrant was a private person while expressing his love for Leyla. He was a little embarrassed by Kamal's friendliness.

"I feel so proud to hear good things from you, Mr. Rana. I wish he keeps doing good work. I am surprised that he has my picture as his PC wallpaper and wish he keeps loving me the way he does right now." Leyla blushed.

"By the way, when are the wedding bells ringing?" Kamal asked.

The question had stuck her hard. It was something that they had never discussed. In fact, 'Are they marrying at all?' was the question she had in mind. She stood still with a blank expression on her face. The smile on her face faded away as she waited for Vikrant to take charge of the conversation. Vikrant looked at her and understood the dilemma Kamal had pushed her in. He held Leyla's hand in his and replied, "Thanks for reminding me

Kamal, I haven't proposed to her yet." He smiled while winking at Leyla.

He rolled his eyes around the hall, calling his close colleagues, Maya and Shahan. He said, "I have to ask Leyla an important question today. I never call her my girlfriend though, I call her my 'big woman', and this will be the last time I would call her that."

Leyla was embarrassed; she felt shy and awkward. Vikrant continued, "Leyla I am a hopeless romantic, but since you are bearing with me…" Vikrant paused and everybody laughed. He continued again, "Bringing flowers and cards look stupid to me. Pre-decided candle light dinner is a cliché. Let me ask you this straight and point blank… will you be my legally wedded wife?" He looked at Leyla who was drenched in emotions. Her deep black eyes were wide with surprise as she looked right through him in amazement.

Leyla kept looking at Vikrant. She had never seen him this happy. For the first time she witnessed him smiling through his eyes. She wandered in his twinkling eyes and couldn't help but answered, "I will, Vikrant. I will. I give my whole life to you." Vikrant jumped in excitement and wrapped her in a warm embrace.

Vikrant's colleagues congratulated the couple with a hearty applause. There were murmurs in the background, "One more wicket down!" While Maya and Shahan came forward and hugged both of them, everybody else got engaged in chatter and watched the dance performances by their colleagues on the stage.

The place was beautifully decorated and filled with happy, positive vibes. Leyla was walking on the beautiful lawn outside the hall, constantly thinking about the moment that had passed a few minutes back. Unexpectedly, she felt that it was too early to get committed for wedding.

What does she know about this man, about Vikrant?

She knows nothing about his family, never met any of them. A cross-cultural wedding! Would his parents, especially his stepmother, be accommodating? Would Leyla be respected? Engulfed in insecurities, she could feel goose bumps. Suddenly, Vikrant's junior, Abdul Ali came to her and said, "Congratulations ma'am. May god bless you both with happiness throughout." Leyla smiled at him and asked, "Thanks! So how do you find him as a boss?"

He gave a strange look at Leyla, took a long pause as if he was deciding what to respond or whether to respond to her at all. After a moment of introspection, he finally spoke, "Unpredictable".

"As in?" Leyla enquired.

"Both as a boss and a human being," he added. There was something disturbing in his expressions, something displeasing, something downright detestable. He moved away from her as if he had hinted something to her and now it was her turn to decode the message. Leyla wanted to talk to him further but his colleagues pulled him into the crowd. Leyla felt helpless and puzzled.

Vikrant noticed Leyla standing alone. He excused himself from the conversations and walked towards her. With his arm resting on her shoulders, he asked, "Hey darling! What is bothering you?"

She looked at him. It took her a moment to shrug off Abdul's opinion and she said, "Marriage is a big decision, Vikrant. What do we know about each other's families? Will they agree? Are we sure to take up this struggle?"

Vikrant smiled at Leyla and replied, "Do you think I will ask you out before ensuring my own commitments? Leyla, it has been three long years since we have been together and you still don't know me, do you?" He took out his cell phone and called his dad. "Hi dad. I hope you are not sleeping?" Leyla was taken by surprise again.

"Hey Vicky, my son! Not at all. But I was not expecting your call at this hour either. You told me you would be busy with the annual day celebration at your office."

"I know, Dad. But I must make you speak to someone. I hope you can guess who. I have asked her hand in marriage, Daddy. She is not sure if you would agree or not." A huge crackling laughter echoed from the other side of his phone. Vikrant put the call on speaker and handed it over to Leyla.

She nervously held the phone and said, "Hi Uncle. How are you doing?"

"Hi Leyla. Dear, my son keeps talking about you all the time. In the last few days, he also spoke to me about his wish to marry you. The more he talks about you, the more I wish to meet you. There is no reason to feel insecure, Leyla. I know about you and the choice which my son has made. Vikrant also emailed me your pictures. You should ask him what I said."

Leyla looked at Vikrant and said, "What?"

"Vikrant chuckled and replied, "He said you look like my mom when she was twenty-one and married him. And mind you, my mom was the most beautiful woman on earth!"

Leyla smiled and said, "Thank you Uncle." The conversation did make her feel reassured. She took a deep breath and smiled.

"Are you making him eat the famous Delhi parathas? I hope you are feeding him well there. Take care, Leyla. And once you guys are ready for marriage, I shall not hesitate to come to Delhi and speak to your parents."

"Sure Uncle, thanks. It's nice speaking to you. Goodnight."

Before Leyla could say anything, Kamal came looking for them, "Hey Vikrant, that's a memento for you. I am sure Leyla will love it." He gave them the gift and went to distribute mementos to other colleagues.

Vikrant opened it and found a coffee mug with his desktop wallpaper (Leyla's picture) printed on it.

The event went off well. Vikrant's presentation on his latest website was appreciated by everyone in the office. His team also received the 'Young innovator of the year' award. After the event ended, all four of them left for Vikrant's house to stay for the night.

The lovers

Leyla took off her sandals and rested on the black leather couch, while Vikrant was preparing steamy hot filter coffee for everyone. This was the first time she had seen Vikrant's apartment. It was the first night that she was spending with him. She felt both nervous and happy at the same time. Vikrant's 2bhk apartment in the posh area of Defence Colony in New Delhi was given to him by his company. The apartment was tastefully decorated with two windows overlooking the large balcony and had a well-equipped kitchen. They enjoyed the aromatic coffee and after a brief chit-chat, Shahan and Maya retired to sleep in the other room.

It was raining more than usual tonight. Leyla was looking outside the window at the sky on the coldest day of the month and listening to Vikrant's deep voice while he was sitting on his favourite wooden armchair, narrating to her some intense lines from *Romeo & Juliet*, "Did my heart love till now? Forswear it, sight! For I never saw true beauty till this night." The room was filled with his husky voice and the crackling sound of bonfire in the middle of the night made Leyla's heart grow fonder.

Her curious brain threw questions at her randomly which she decided to ask later and continued to soak herself in the magical spell of his voice. But one stubborn question had stuck her rather hard and she finally interrupted the unbroken voice of Vikrant with her gentle yet inquisitive voice… "Vicky, were Romeo and Juliet soulmates?"

Although Vikrant was taken aback by Leyla's sudden question, he rather chose to answer it! "Dame, only soulmates are able to die for each other, and to die together, isn't it simple?" Leyla smiled and silently admired Vikrant's ability of simplifying complexities of life with this ease.

"How does he do it every time? How does he simply unlock my brain inch by inch and makes me understand complicated things in the blink of his eye? He is just marvellous, in every sense, in every way. He is everything I ever wanted and imagined." She thought to herself and remained glued to his voice as he continued to read. Leyla was lost in her thoughts and fell fast asleep inside Vikrant's embrace. He stopped reading as he felt Leyla's deep breath which usually signified her uninterrupted sleep after a long tiring day. He had often listened this deep breath over the phone during late night conversations, whenever she fell asleep in the middle of their conversation. He would whisper "good night" and carefully disconnect the call. Next day, he would tease her with playful words, "My doll snores! Well actually she does a little more than breathing, little less than snoring!" Leyla would feel embarrassed, bang the phone on his face and would not pick his call for some time.

He had known her so well only by listening to her voice during all these years. Today, he could finally see her sleeping, right in front of him.

Vikrant softly touched Leyla's eyes to see if the gateway to his world was shut in peace. He loved to see her sleeping softly and kept staring at her for a long while.

Slowly he lifted her in his arms with her head placed carefully on his chest. He took her to the bed and tucked her in with a soft maroon blanket. He kissed her forehead and murmured "I love you, my darling angel, good night". Leyla returned his gesture by smiling in her sleep. That was the depth of Leyla's love for Vikrant and his influence on her life. He could make her hear him even when she was in a deep slumber!

Leyla woke up with the noise of lightning bolts and thunder. It was still dark outside. As she stepped on the marble floor, out from her warm caressing blanket, she shivered with cold. She walked across the room and stood close to the fireplace where fire was almost extinguished but the wooden platform was still warm and comfortable. Her eyes were stuck on Vikrant's face. He was sleeping on his back, facing her, with his legs overlapping the set of cushions. Leyla admired the innocence that reflected from his face as she lay on the black leather couch placed opposite the armchair to catch up another short nap before the day began. Her mind took her back, to wander in the lanes of the past where they both had interacted for the first time.

First encounter

Vikrant's first encounter with Leyla happened online, when he was working in the US and she was a final year student of graduation in Mumbai. Both had participated in a blog writing competition, on an interesting topic "Beauty Incarnate". While replying to another participant 'A myth', Vikrant had made the most outlandish observations about life and equation of karmas. Leyla was instantly impressed by his choice of words and the way he had put forward his ideas about coincidences that occur in human life. Her curiosity about this enigmatic character was growing, but she still hesitated to look at the strange display picture of his profile on a social networking website. It was a horrifying black monster holding a knife-like object in his hands! Despite being scared, she convinced her mind to explore this mysterious individual and asked him a direct question on his user handle *"@Vikrant: What is life in your opinion and how should it be lived?"* Vikrant's reply on her question astonished Leyla. It seemed as if he had known her for a long time.

@Leyla:

Seek within
deep inside
it's not the world around
nor the dirt on the ground
it's not life that gives you
it's you who gets the due
hard to understand I feel
about the hand in deal
life comes with no value
listen now as I tell you
it's not how life is beautiful
but a beauty so dutiful
on a way seems lost
with everything put to cost
soon as hay burns in fast
cometh winter that to last
not in time to wait to be
but to run and break free
as when does strike boredom
calm thyself and roar for freedom.
Posted @10:45 P.M.

@Vikrant: Thanks for the prompt reply. What a beautiful way of weaving your thoughts into poetry! I am sure I have no dearth of questions to ask and hope you would not mind answering them time and again.

Posted @10:48 P.M.

@Leyla: Pleasure is all mine, sweet lady. I am new to this blog and I am honored to receive a friendly welcome from you all. It's like a new family away from a family for me. Good night folks! Adios…

Posted @10:50 P.M.

That night, Leyla slept thinking about 'Mr. Mystery' and dreamt about rivers, rains, hills and oceans. She was sitting with Vikrant on the seashore while having an endless conversation. They were giggling and making castles in the sand. Next morning, Leyla woke up with a smile on her face. She was more cheerful than usual the entire day. She was blushing and was eager to share her dream with Vikrant. But she found it too silly as both were complete strangers. Hence, she had roped the idea of any informal communication with this man.

Leyla's memories were interrupted with the ringing of Vikrant's alarm. He woke up, snoozed the alarm clock and saw Leyla sitting on the black leather couch. He slowly walked towards her and held her softly from behind.

"What are you doing here so early, honey? Did you sleep well last night?"

"Yes. I slept well, woke up fresh and wandered in the lanes of the past."

"Really! What all did you think about?" He held her close and kissed her softly.

"I was thinking about how we met online and spent two long years in a long-distance relationship. How you relocated from USA to Delhi to be with me last month and how you proposed me for marriage last night! It's all like a dream Vicky, like a dream journey. I am living a perfect fairy tale." Leyla was caressing him while Vikrant played with her hair.

"Darling, tell me how did you like my father?" poised Vikrant.

"Oh, he is amazing. I felt as if I have known him since a long time. Vikrant, when are you planning to meet my dad? When shall I break this news to them?" She paused and asked.

"Not now, Leyla. We will have to wait for at least one year. I need to finish this project and work on getting my visa for the US again. Once I am done with that, we will meet your father." He kept kissing Leyla while replying.

"Work out the visa for the US? But it should be your company's responsibility if they will send you for any project there." Leyla turned around and looked straight into Vikrant's eyes.

"Yes, but only if I get another project in the US, otherwise, they will hold me up in India for their monotonous work. In that case, I will join another company to go to US," he replied calmly.

"I see. But, I am okay to live in India too, close to our parents. Why do we have to leave them and go to the USA?" She was not convinced with Vikrant's response.

"Leyla, you have no idea! Life is very easy there. Rich and smooth. It will be good for me to live there and I have decided to settle in the US only." He raised his voice slightly to make his point clear.

"Okay. I won't argue if it's so important for you." Leyla gave up and walked away from Vikrant.

"Sweetheart, I can ensure that with me, you will lead a rich life, but not a stable one," Vikrant said in a softer tone.

"In what context?" Leyla posed a question at him again.

"Like some ladies have these emotional attachments with their house and things. But, I like to change places, in almost every two years. I keep changing cities and thankfully my work allows me this mobility," he said

"Vikrant, it's great till a point, but beyond that, you need stability. You can't keep changing your child's school every year." Leyla was getting impatient with this new revelation about future.

"I don't know how will you manage, Leyla. But with me, mobility or instability, however you wish to interpret, will always remain a part of our life. I hate to be caged. I prefer changing the city when my social circle in the same city expands and passes the threshold. I don't like unnecessary attachments and friendships." Vikrant spoke in a dismissing way, as if these were his final words and there was no scope of any further discussion on this topic.

Leyla felt awkward but chose to end the discussion and said, "We will cross the bridge as and when it will appear." There was an awkward silence between them. His words were still ringing in her ears. Why does he hate to be unveiled? What is so secretive about him that he doesn't want people to discover? Why does he still appear to be a total stranger to her? Why does he scare her to the core sometimes? What did Abdul mean by Vikrant being unpredictable?

She had known him for couple of years now, and yet, there were layers of enigma around him. He sometimes gave away strong feeling of deformity in his mind, although she couldn't clearly see what it was. She was indebted to him. He had mentored her during her tough years, pulled her out of the darkness of her circumstances, transformed her into an independent and courageous woman, and yet, she couldn't totally fathom him at all. His unforthcoming and self-contained tendencies had always been the reason to worry for Leyla.

The eerie silence in the room was broken by the knock on their door. Maya and Shahan were awake too. Leyla quickly got up and opened the door. Maya greeted them with morning wishes and asked Leyla to get ready to go home, where they could get ready and reach office on time.

On the job

"How could I do this? This is height of carelessness. Egg-headed moron of highest order. Damn foolish I am!" Leyla kept cursing herself while getting ready for office because she had left her diary and wallet at Vikrant's house. This was for the Nth time that she had misplaced her things. This behaviour was analogous with Leyla. Whenever her mother sulked over her disorganised ways, she would quickly quip, "God-gifted children are always unorganized." This made her skip the long lectures coming her way.

In her heart, she knew that her mother's concerns were right in her own limited knowledge, but she was a gifted thinker and knew that she had to bear the drawbacks of going awry, being unorganized and experiencing mental fatigue. With the twenty-third year of her life, she had come to terms with her shortcomings. She was a dreamer, a poet, a thinker. Leyla knew that fitting in this world of practical organized cowards would always be a struggle for her.

She picked her bag, a pen, notepad and ran off after gulping the breakfast which was already prepared by her mother, without letting her find out that Leyla had misplaced something again. It was her first day in office after her training period had gotten over only last week. She never wanted to spoil her mood with long lectures now.

As she boarded the metro, Vikrant called up, "Good morning, my big woman! Wish you all the best."

"Hey! Morning Vicky. Thanks a ton."

"Now listen to me before you interrupt. It's not a college that you are joining. That's the bloody ruthless corporate world. Okay! You will not make friends there. Aim high. Be ahead of your colleagues in vision and actions and focus on your job. Half of your colleagues will misguide you, will try to distract you and push you off the track, while they will be focusing strongly on their objectives all this while. Besides that, there will be sadists and morons who will feel that the company is misusing them, underpaying them and there is no growth in the organization. But listen to me darling, such people are nothing more than stinking pieces of shit. They don't want to move their ass and work. Ask about their performance and they'll have thousand reasons to blame the product for nonperformance. Check their knowledge and you will be surprised and think how they managed to be managers, they should rather be mopping floors from their face. I love you darls. That's all I had to say. Now you can interrupt."

"Vikrant, you need to calm down first." Leyla burst into a loud laughter. She controlled her laughter when she realized people around were looking at her and continued, "Vicky, I am inducted in you. You will always know when to grab me from my neck and get me back. I love you Vicky. I know I am vulnerable darling, but trust me, now I am getting better. And seriously, do not freak out. I won't be blowing off my chance. Ok! Now relax and go to office. See you in the evening. Bye."

"Of course! I need to meet you to give your belongings back to you. Things which you had carelessly left at my place yesterday. Bye!"

Leyla knew where Vikrant's concerns were coming from. Vikrant had invested a lot of time in pulling her out of the black hole which was sucking her life endlessly. He was proud to see Leyla turned into this confident woman now. Vikrant was over cautious of keeping Leyla away from grief and setbacks; all he wanted was to see her taking charge of her life independently.

Leyla stepped out of the metro and took the escalator to exit the station. Despite having grown up in Delhi, she had come to the interiors of Barakhamba for the first time. During her previous visits to Connaught Place, she would see high rise buildings from a distance, but never got a chance to walk on these premier streets ever before. Connaught Place is a circular shopping complex named after George V's Uncle, the Duke of Connaught. The whitewashed streets majorly harbour popular bars, international stores and a few book shops which are immune to the lost glory of bookstores in general.

While Barakhamba Road and KG Marg are the biggest commercial centres of Delhi. These premier streets are beautiful but have modern day buildings standing tall on both sides of the road. She was amazed to see beautiful upscale architecture that surrounded her on all sides. Leyla was fascinated by The Statesman House, especially after reading the story behind the name tag of this famous road. It was credited to the twelve-pillared house of a noble man, which was orginally built on this road during the rule of Sultan Mohammad Tuglaq. History can be demolished, but cannot be erased. She wanted to get inside the building and have a look around, but she rushed towards the Vijaya building where she was supposed to report to her office on the eighth floor.

Maya was already waiting for her at the entrance of the building. "Hey! I was about to call you. It's a damn cold morning and I am freezing here, waiting for you." Maya hugged Leyla.

"Yeah! The chilly winds are killer, babes. Sorry for being late as usual. Old habits die hard, you see." They giggled and took the lift to the eighth floor.

When they entered the premises, their zonal head, Mr. Aman Malik was already standing at the entrance of the lobby and was talking on his sparkling iPhone 7. He looked at both the girls and shifted his gaze to the Tissot Aqua Terra which graced his wrist. He kept his phone aside and muttered, "It's 9:38 a.m. Next time, please do not stretch it beyond 9:30 a.m." Aman Malik was a short, young and fit man in a light pink shirt with black cufflinks. The black tie around his collar complemented his well-fitted black trousers. Leyla felt embarrassed, while a warning on the first day puzzled Maya. She never expected him to be uncompromising even for eight minutes. She murmured playfully in Leyla's ears, "You are dead! Aman is punctual, err… in your words he is a clock-watcher. How will you handle it, Leyla? You better resign today itself."

"Shut up! I am seriously dead! Find me another job," she replied. They looked at each other and broke into a liberating laughter as they passed the lobby area.

The premise was magnificently designed and fully-furnished with around sixty workstations. The glass cabins were spacious and beautiful. Both of them had just placed their bags inside one of the free cubicles inside the hall, when Mr. Malik entered and called everybody inside his cabin. The office was lavishly decorated with one glass wall in each hall. This was a window to the magnificent Barakhamba Street. As Leyla entered Mr. Malik's cabin, her gaze traversed the room and got fixed on the beautiful portrait of modern art which was mounted on the wall behind his chair. She was also intrigued by the coffee mug on the table. It had a quote which said, 'A winner never whines'.

Aman sat on his long black swivel chair and sipped his morning tea while addressing his team, "Good morning team! We have two new joinees with us today, Miss. Leyla Rajput and Maya Singh. They have just finished their MBA. I expect you guys to help them understand our business and products. Leyla and Maya, every morning, we start with our morning huddle at 9:30 a.m. and discuss the agendas and priorities for the day. So, make sure you reach office before 9:30 a.m. Now please introduce yourself to the team and we shall take the meeting forward." He opened his laptop and continued sipping his tea.

Leyla took the lead and said, "Hi all. Since you all already know my name and qualification, I will keep it short and crisp. I was born in Mumbai and brought up in Delhi. Hopefully, I will learn a great deal here. Thanks."

Aman sarcastically interrupted, "I hope you realize that you are out of school. You have to implement here what you have already learnt."

"Oh yes! I understand that." Leyla felt embarrassed for the second time that day; it was not a good start. However, Aman was smiling at her notoriously; he was gauging her potential in his own witty style. Aman was known to be a thorough professional and an arduous task master. He would assign work and clients to people based on their interpersonal skills, stress management skills and endurance. He had been awarded the 'Best Leader' trophy by his company during the last two consecutive years.

Maya also introduced herself and the meeting was quickly directed towards team agendas. Before dispersing the meeting, Mr. Malik told Leyla, "Enjoy the honeymoon period in the corporate culture. You just need to get your email ID configured and interact with the team members today. You should accompany them for client meetings during the next ten days. But after that, you must gear yourself up to handle target pressures. All the best girls and welcome to JSM investment bank's family."

Maya and Leyla got their IDs configured and chit-chatted with the entire team. While some of them frightened the girls with work pressure, the others advised them to work smart and get noticed. Leyla was fascinated to hear stories of clients and how some of them are now good friends and were giving good business opportunities to the organisation. The excitement made Leyla eager to share her experiences with Vikrant. After everyone had left for their respective meetings, she called Vikrant but quickly disconnected when she saw Mr. Malik coming towards them. He noticed the girls and asked Maya, "No lunch for you?" Leyla quickly disconnected the call and replied, "Yes, we will go.".

"We usually bring home-cooked food. You can join in case you want to share. You can also ask the pantry guys to bring you food from outside. We have many options here."

"We were thinking if we can walk down and grab something from Subway," Leyla replied.

He laughed and replied, "Yes, you sure can, but only till your honeymoon period lasts. After that you won't be able to afford it due to work pressure."

He smirked and walked away.

Leyla was now sure that Aman was a sarcastic boss. He always had this smirk on his face while talking to her. The more she disliked him, the more she believed that there was a lot to learn from him.

Leyla was grabbing her bag when her phone rang. It was Vikrant. "Hi darling, what's up with you. I am sorry for disconnecting the call," she said.

"That's ok Leyla. I am on the way to CP with my trainer. He had some work here. I thought I would also roam around a bit and was wondering if you could join in for a quick lunch. Only if only you can manage with ease."

"Wow Vicky!!! What a coincidence. Maya and I were just stepping out to grab a bite. Can't believe that you are here. How much time do you have?"

"He has some friend from his country who works with the Spain commercial office here. He is meeting him over a cup of coffee at The Lalit. So I guess I have one hour."

"Cool! Same here. I can easily come out for an hour. But Maya is also with me. I hope you won't mind."

"Aaaahhhh, you know what I want. But, alas, bring her along!"

"Where are we meeting?"

"At The Lalit."

Maya's dilemma

Leyla and Maya were waiting for Vikrant in the hotel lobby. He entered the lobby with Fernando in a white linen shirt paired with faded blue denims, brown belt and brown woodland shoes. He looked stunning. His looks make Leyla blush. His tall broad silhouette overshadowed Fernando's sophisticated personality. As they walked closer, Vikrant winked at Leyla and flashed a wide contagious smile. Leyla's face turned crimson. Maya noticed their chemistry and pressed Leyla's hand to tease her, "Can I date him for a day?" she said.

"Shut up!" Leila pinched her and laughed. Maya had always been impressed by Vikrant's personality, though she had hardly met him. She remembered when they had met in CP with Shahan at a random Chinese restaurant where Vikrant had invited them. Leyla had told her about Vikrant's wisdom and the story of a mentor who had turned into a lover. Maya felt a connection with him in that first meeting.

Maya was still lost in memories when Vikrant turned towards Maya and said, "Maya, it's nice to see you again."

"Hi Vikrant! Nice to see you too." She couldn't stop giggling.

"By the way, he is Fernando, our trainer. And Fernando, she is Leyla, my girlfriend and her friend Maya."

"Hello beauties! Wish I could spend more time with you. But alas, a friend is waiting for me in the cafe. I will need your permission to leave."

"Sure Fernando. Nice to see you."

"Take care Vikrant and have fun with your girl. Will catch you both soon."

While Fernando left for the café, they walked into the coffee shop and settled in one of the tables. The place was cheerful with a lot of conversations in the background. Vikrant looked at the wide range of items on the menu. He was delighted to see American and Chinese cuisine. Exploring the city with his lady love made him love his stay in Delhi. But he missed American food. Without a second thought, he ordered a Caesar salad with Ptarmigan-Reggiano, burger and fries with lemon ice tea. He looked at both the girls and asked for their order. Maya was surprised and said, "Looking at the number of dishes you just ordered, I thought you have already ordered for us."

Vikrant laughed at Maya and asked Leyla. "Leyla, you didn't tell her about my appetite? I am a voracious eater, dear Maya. That order is for me alone. You both can decide your respective dishes since I am not going to share mine, even a bit."

Maya was stunned at his bluntness, but Leyla kept laughing. She said, "Darling, don't be offended. He is rough with words at times, but a gem of a person."

Vikrant retorted at Leyla, "I am a gem only for you, Leyla! Not to be taken for granted by all, "Then he turned towards

Maya and continued," I am like a mirror Maya. I reflect people's realities at them and they get hurt sometimes."

Maya confidently looked at Vikrant and said, "I appreciate that. I would want to see my reality, Vikrant. I hope I could learn something from you. In fact, I wanted to ask if you could guide me through a situation I am in."

"I charge! My advice doesn't come for free." Vikrant spoke in a rather stern tone and paused. Maya was once again taken aback by his hostile remarks.

Leyla snapped at Vikrant, "Vicky! Stop scaring her off now."

Leyla never liked this unaccommodating behaviour of his. She understood that he had lived a troubled childhood due to the early demise of his mother and the unruly behaviour of his stepmother. He learnt to deal with emotional hardships by "toughening up" and appearing cold to people he did not know much about. It was his defense mechanism. His cold personality did not make him any less human though. He was caring and sensitive for the people he loved. But Leyla knew Maya very well. She was fond of her and wanted Vikrant to understand that Maya would not harm him in any way.

Vikrant chuckled while Maya's bewildered and perplexed expressions were noticeable. Vikrant looked at Maya's big deep eyes and understood there was more to her than what could be seen on the surface. She did not just please Vikrant, but rather needed his help. He realized that an untold story was suffocating Maya. He was probably the first person she was trying to open up with. Vikrant felt like explaining to her that she was expecting a bit too much from him as he was just hosting her for lunch since she was Leyla's close friend and now, an office colleague too.

"Maya, I am not a friendly person. I can't comfort strangers. But you are Leyla's friend and I have regards for you. There is nothing more to it. By the way, what do you want to learn from me? We are just acquaintances." Vikrant explained to her, point blank.

Maya replied," Vikrant, I know Leyla since childhood. She has always been an inspiration. She was one of the sharpest students in school. I don't know what went wrong, but her performance and confidence both wilted with time. But you have helped her have her confidence back. That undoubtedly makes you a man of wisdom. Leyla respects very few people. I know her standards as well as her choice."

"I am honored Maya, but what can I teach you? I am not a motivational speaker, nor am I a social worker. I am only a software engineer who is earning to make ends meet and grow in life." He spoke while relishing his lemon iced tea.

"I am going through a confusing phase, Vikrant. I need some advice," answered Maya.

"Oh, I see. Go on. I will help you to the best of my knowledge."

"Shall I speak now? I hope I am not spoiling your lunch date?" Maya hesitated.

Leyla lashed out at Maya. "Stop being a crack-nut and speak up. This date won't be of any worth if you go home with a burdened heart."

Maya's eyes turned misty as she spoke, "I love Shahan a lot. But he is a Muslim and I hail from a strict Hindu family. My parents will disown me if they get to know about this relationship. But we have been in love since ten long years. We were both thirteen, I guess."

"Aha!" Vikrant was listening to her carefully while the food arrived.

"You already know he is leaving for California in a couple of months for his MBA. And before that, he wants to know if he is committed to me for marriage," she continued.

"You are of the same age. Why think of doing an MBA now?" Vikrant posed.

"He was working in a MNC. It was an entry level job. But he wants a higher salary package to give me a decent life. Though he can't match my father's financial status, he is trying that we lead a comfortable life, if not luxurious."

"Why can't he match your father's financial stature? Why are you underestimating your own love?" asked Vikrant.

Leyla interrupted in between and said, "Vikrant it's not about underestimating Shahan. I think I haven't told you. Her father has six textile mills. He drives an Audi. She drives a BMW. Her brother a Merc."

"Really?? Why are you working here? Why don't you join your dad's business?" Vikrant asked. He was rather surprised now, after knowing her financial background.

Maya answered, rather hesitatingly, "Well, we share a turbulent and estranged relationship. His violence during my childhood has made me an indifferent daughter today. I think we both hate each other."

Vikrant was baffled. "I see. There are strange people here. Somebody's getting harassed within the family, somebody getting smashed by father. A colleague told me that his brother is an alcoholic and tried to molest her the other night. She was lucky to have eloped and stays as a PG now. Leyla, South India is a very different place. We are conservative yet modern, educated and value-oriented families."

Leyla fuddled, "Chuck it, Vicky! Not everyone is like that. Maya, tell us how do you think we can help?"

"See, if I decide to marry him, eloping is the only way out. I understand I am blinded by love and can't see which way to go. Leave my family behind or leave my love behind… I want you guys to decide for me," Maya said.

"But a ten-year-old relationship should be mature enough to decide that." Vikrant raised his eyebrows at Maya.

"No Vikrant. We have had many break-ups during this journey. But we patched up every time since we couldn't stay away for long. I find him immature and he feels that I am aggressive and impatient," she spoke in a dejected tone.

"How attached are you with your family?" Vikrant posed again.

"My father is biased and favours my brother. Gender biased, I feel. My mother never protected me when I was getting smashed by him. I don't think I am attached to her either." She was embarrassed, yet she answered Vikrant frankly.

"And with Shahan?" Vikrant continued posing questions at her.

"He is my first love. I find my family in him."

"That's it! Your decision is already taken. I just need to approve it and seal it with my stamp. So when are we meeting him again?" Vikrant asked while eating.

"Wow! Let's meet this weekend. Let's make it a random meeting. He should not know why we are meeting." A smiling curve appeared on Maya's face as she expressed her gratitude for Vikrant.

"Done. Leyla, you decide the place and time. A fascinating place for me, please. So that if I reject Shahan, I will at least have a good place to spend my weekend." Vikrant joked while feeding Leyla from his plate.

Leyla was amused. She laughingly scolded, "Vikrant!! You are too rude at times."

"I am not a pleaser, darling. Get used to me," Vikrant said. He held Leyla closer to him and kissed her forehead.

Destiny

Leyla was flipping through her visiting card holder. She had met the owner of a private limited company at a seminar, a couple of days back. Aman asked her to fix an appointment with the prospect client for presentation of their products at his office. She was trying to recall his name and was cursing herself for not penning it down. Aman came to her desk and asked, "Did you call Mr. Oberoi from HMBL LTD?" He was the same guy whose name Leyla was trying to recollect.

She surprisingly looked at him and smiled at him for a few seconds. Aman raised his eyebrow at her in awkwardness and asked again, "Did you?"

Leyla quickly pulled herself back from the amusement and cooked up a lie," Yes, I called, but he was in a meeting. He has asked me to call him back at 1 p.m. It's ten minutes to 1. I will update you accordingly."

Aman nodded and moved towards his cabin. She exhaled her breath and laid back on her chair in relief. She never preferred lying, but in situations like this, she believed that 'a small lie never hurt anyone'! She repeated this to herself and continued her search for Mr. Oberoi's visiting card. She was amazed at these coincidences of life and wondered how life gets to know what we need and when.

Mr. Oberoi asked her to visit his office in Hauz Khas at 5 p.m. She asked her branch manager to accompany her, but he was leaving early that evening. She hesitatingly asked Aman if he could accompany her for the meeting. Aman was the CEO and the branch managers reported to him. He was keen on meeting clients, but met them only if the deal had potential. First round of meetings was usually done by branch managers and managers. Leyla could have handled the meeting alone too, but she was still new and not prepared for handling the FAQs. Hence, Aman agreed to accompany her.

Leyla drove to the meeting in her own car as she wanted to leave for home after finishing the meeting. After the meeting, Leyla offered to drop Aman to the nearest metro station so that he could go back to office to pick his car. She was aware that Aman was a workaholic and preferred to work till 9 p.m. The meeting stretched for a couple of hours. Aman desperately wanted to have some coffee and a smoke. He requested Leyla to stop at the nearest coffee shop if she was not running late. Leyla stopped at a Café Coffee Day on the way. As they both sat on a table, Leyla noticed Aman's restlessness. She hesitatingly asked him, "Are you ok sir?"

"Oh yes! I am. I just wanted a smoke, would you mind if I take a quick drag and come back."

"Yes sure! Please go ahead."

Leyla was exhausted too. It was not the meeting that exhausted them, but Mr. Oberoi's cunning personality that annoyed them more. He was a true businessman who negotiated hard, relentlessly. It was challenging to keep smiling and not hurt his ego during the process. Aman was back in a few minutes and laughed, "Oh Gosh! He tested my patience, man!"

Leyla smiled and nodded in agreement.

"But you know, that's what clients teach you. Endurance. It bends your ego and makes you flexible," Aman continued.

"But there was a point where I just wanted to walk out from his office. He was so sarcastic and spoke as if we were asking for a personal favour! Like we went to borrow money from him." Leyla exclaimed.

"Haha. Leyla, you would see yourself after five years from now. You will be ruthless and manipulative like him in meetings. You would know how to manage a tough customer like him." Aman pacified her.

"Oh yes! I could see how you were handling him with so much ease. But then, why are you so restlessness now?" Leyla asked Aman in a calm tone.

"Oh, that was my urge to smoke. Now I am fine. I usually smoke every 30 minutes." Aman confessed.

"But that's harmful," She hesitated but managed to voice her concern.

"That's a cliché." Aman shrugged off Leyla's concern. "Anyway, I hope you are enjoying work."

"Yes. Do you still enjoy work after being in this trade for so long?" Leyla counter-questioned.

"It's an addiction, Leyla! Work becomes an obsession, not a means of reaching a goal after you've climbed the ladder and acquired senior positions," Aman said.

Leyla looked at his tired face. In office, Aman was the most energetic leader. But here in front of her, he took off that mask and revealed a different version of him. Leyla had never imagined that he would also have this side to his personality.

Leyla questioned him further, "But do you think this is your destiny, sir?"

"No. My destiny lies somewhere else," Aman replied without looking at Leyla. He could not face Leyla at that moment. It was as if he was the culprit who showed these young professionals a rosy picture of corporate life, but right at this moment, he could not hide the truth.

"But have you discovered your true purpose?" Leyla continued asking.

She had mixed emotions. She was in a tizzy to see Aman in this state and was confused about her own destiny now. She empathised with him, but was also surrounded by an urgency to find a new meaning for her life. She would never want to see herself in Aman's shoes, ten years down the line.

"Yes. I have discovered it. I have tracked my destiny, yet waiting to trap it." He laughed in his own notorious style.

"What are you waiting for?" Leyla continued.

"Waiting to find out how to make the leap without jeopardizing things like home, family and my sanity." He smiled and took the last sip from his cup and asked for the cheque. He hurriedly swiped his card and made way for Leyla to walk out. Leyla wanted to spend more time though, she wanted to know his ambitions, his success story, his plans to reach his goals. She had this burning urge to learn from people with substance, from books, from experiences, from life. She had not yet discovered her true potential and destiny. But there was this uneasiness in her which she knew would settle only once she would meet her destiny, find her true calling. She wanted to see what is unseen and wanted to think the unthinkable. She was the child of curiosity. But holding her emotions back, Leyla wished him a happy weekend and drove back home.

Good times

"Wake up, Leyla! Its 11 a.m. What are you up to?" Leyla's mom made a third attempt to wake her up. She woke up startled and realized that she was on phone with Vikrant till 6 a.m. She got out of the bed with a wide smile. She could recollect the mawkish conversations which they had. "Oh! How much more will I love you Vicky? You are irresistible!" she murmured and rushed to get ready.

Maya called her, "Leyla, where the hell are you? I have been calling you since 9 a.m. Goddammit! We guys are meeting for lunch I suppose, and it's 12 already!" Maya was yelling from the other side of the phone.

"Yes. I am almost ready. I will pick you up from your place in fifteen minutes. Vikrant will join us in Vasant Vihar. What about Shahan?" Leyla tried to pacify her.

"He is going to reach The China House by 1 p.m." Maya was still speaking loudly.

"Oh crap! We are late. We will take at least one and a half hours to reach," Leyla finally realized that she won't make it on time.

"No Leyla, we are not late …you are late as usual." Maya disconnected the call in exasperation.

"Guys, I am hungry and so are you all. Let's order first," Vikrant said while looking hurriedly at the menu.

Shahan pulled his chair and bent backwards. He had a beautiful face. Shahan was a handsome man with sophisticated body language. Maya leaned on his shoulder and kept looking at Vikrant, hopeful of his approval. Leyla pulled her by the arm and murmured in her ears, "I will let you date Vikrant for one day in bargain of you letting me date Shahan for a month at least."

Maya whispered back, "Only after getting married to them. Otherwise they will call off the weddings after discovering the badass women that we are." They both started laughing at their little joke.

"Share the joke ladies," Vikrant asked curiously.

"I am sure it's a dirty one." Shahan spoke while hugging Maya tightly.

"Well yes, a little dirty. Maybe you can guess. Maybe we will let you figure out our billion dollar proposal in future!" Maya said playfully.

"I hope the ladies are not inspired from *Indecent Proposal*," Vikrant spoke in his style while sipping his beer.

"Oh my god! Maya, they are getting closer, keep quiet now," Leyla continued the joke.

"In that case, I hope I am the one making the offer and not being the offer itself," Vikrant teased her.

"Shut up guys! I am already feeling homesick. I am going to miss the fun. And look at you enjoying my farewell party." Shahan laughed.

Vikrant and Shahan got along well. They talked about America and education abroad. Vikrant gave him tips to survive in America. Shahan found him interesting and mature. After lunch, Vikrant helped Shahan to buy clothes as per the weather in California.

Coffee was served along with muffins. Leyla's jaw was hurting after all that laughter. It was a perfect weekend. Leyla suddenly realized that her life was so perfect at this moment. Her best friend was sitting by her side and her love in front of her eyes. From complete darkness, life had come to this beautiful moment. Vikrant noticed her misty eyes and instantly messaged her. *"Darling, I love you. Nothing will go wrong from here. Have no fear, okay!"*

Leyla was amazed about how Vikrant does that every time. How did he get to know what's going on in her mind, what she fears and how to deal with it! Leyla smiled back in gratitude. She felt indebted towards this man and thought if she could love him enough in this lifetime and give him all the happiness he deserves. She doubted and a killing void filled her. Just then she received another message from Vikrant, *"You are my only family. You complete me. You keep the devil in me under control and keep me on human planes. Never underestimate the power of your love for me."*

This time Leyla looked up in total surprise and asked him upfront, "Tell me how you know every time?" hence interrupting the ongoing conversation. They all looked perplexed and echoed, "What?!"

Vikrant blushed and said, "Because you are inducted in me."

Shahan and Maya smiled, thinking that they won't know what's going on.

Shahan smiled at the lovely pair and asked, "I want to know how you guys met. You are such a lovely couple. "

Vikrant laughed, "You won't believe, but we met through the internet. There was this blog where many likeminded people used to interact almost daily, mostly during the night. Leyla, you remember the whole gang?"

Leyla replied, "Of course I do. I still have the conversations saved in my email."

"For how long did you chat over internet? And how and when did you first meet?" Shahan was curious to know more.

"We chatted for over two years via internet. Then Vikrant decided to relocate to Delhi. It's a long story Shahan. If we start now, we will end up spending the whole night here." Leyla blushed.

"I am still curious Leyla. Let's go back, I want to hear the story," Shahan insisted.

They got up and moved towards their car. Maya volunteered to drive while Leyla sat with her in the front seat. Shahan sat behind. Vikrant took their leave as his house was in a different direction.

Flashback

Maya was driving while Leyla was looking outside the window. The music was soft. The cold wind caressed her face while she relaxed and watched other vehicles flashing by their side. Shahan insisted that Leyla narrate her story and how Vikrant decided to move to Delhi.

She finally agreed to share it with Shahan.

Avi and Leyla were seeing each other for a couple of years now. But their relationship lacked substance. They were family friends, and knew each other well since childhood days. The bonding between their families, common culture and values which they shared, made their affair natural, almost inevitable. The families went for outings together, to hill stations, to beaches. Parents were aware and in agreement with their relationship. It was the most obvious choice for both families, and Avi. He was a fun-loving man. Appearances mattered to him. He was impressed with Leyla's physical beauty and was handsome and careful about his looks. His idea of a content life was to have Leyla by his side, his friends, and money in his pocket, enough to afford a good lifestyle, to party and get drunk! But Leyla needed much more from life. She was intense. She never disregarded the importance of money, but her idea of money was a means to accomplish bigger things in life. Money is a means, not an end. Leyla wanted to create a legacy. Something like, employ thousands of youth by establishing a corporate with ethics and social responsibility. She would dream of a huge library where she would innovate with ideas to bring back reading habits in people and preserve ancient knowledge and literature. She dreamt of a utopian world.

Sometimes Leyla thought her dreams were unrealistic. So she would decide to simply be the best version of herself. Leyla thought that her ideas were vague, but she was always introspective and retrospective, always looking out for new dimensions of life. She believed in new learnings with every passing day. Leyla yearned for an intense and passionate partner in the journey of life. She loved Avi, but it was almost impossible for her to spend her entire life with him. Avi was also slowly accepting Leyla' detachment from the relationship. The relationship was drifting towards a silent death. It was not that Avi didn't try to mend the differences. He gave more than he could to see a smile on Leyla's face. But eventually he realised that Leyla did not need what he had to offer. In fact, she disliked all that. The only possibility of survival of this relationship was Avi turning into somebody he was not. It no longer seemed plausible; he was stepping back too! It was tragic and painful for both to endure. This phase left them both confused and dejected.

On a hot humid afternoon, Leyla came back from college and took a short nap. After a while she realized she was too stressed to sleep. She missed her meal and in hope to find some diversion online, she logged-in from her desktop. As she signed in to the portal 'Beauty Incarnate', she discovered that a new topic had taken the attention of all the members; "What is love?" It was painful for her to read the word 'love'. She was about to log off, when she saw Vikrant's post, "Love is the epitome of human emotions...you are truly in love when the other person reflects A to Z of what you are, the one who is your own extension. People say opposite attracts, but have you ever heard them say that opposites last too? It's the similarities that keep a relationship going even in rough times, because in such relations, there is an effortless understanding and empathy towards each other."

Leyla contemplated on the above statement in perspective of her relationship with Avi. 'There is nothing common between me and Avi. We are poles apart. But I do care for him. I would go out of my way to see him happy. If what Vikrant is saying is true, then what is between me and Avi?' Her train of thoughts was interrupted when 'A myth' pinged her on chat messenger:

A myth: Leyla, the members of Beauty Incarnate are of a view that we should initiate a group voice chat in the messenger here so that they get a chance to personally know each other. What is your take as a moderator of this thread?

Leyla: I think it's a good idea. Makes sense too. Members have conversed a lot on the thread and we should now take the conversations to another level.

A myth: So, should I initiate this or would you want to invite the members?

Leyla: Please carry on. I have had an exhausting day and will join you in some time.

A myth: No problem. I will manage the chat session. But I suggest that you join. People are very enthusiastic and have plans to sing and recite poetry. This will rejuvenate you.

Leyla: Ok. Give me a moment.

A myth: Sure Leyla. You better have a cup of hot cappuccino.

Leyla: Thanks :)

A myth joins conference call.

Leyla joins conference call.

Karan joins conference call.

Jigar joins conference call.

Ronit joins conference call.

Karan: Hey all!

Leyla: :)

A myth: Hi Leyla and Grey! How are you doing today?

Jigar: Hey all…good afternoon folks!

Ronit: Yoyo;-)

Kamakhya joins conference call.

Pit joins conference call.

Illian join conference call.

A myth: Welcome folks!

Pit : Voila! Here I enter the virtual club "Beauty Incarnate"

Kamakhya: Rofl @ Pit. What an entry!

Karan: How many of you have Mic? I am connecting my speakers.

Voice chat initiated.

A myth: Leyla, are you ok? I am afraid you don't seem fine. Why don't you join the voice chat?

Leyla: Hey ya. Just a little headache. Will join in after having coffee!

V.R joins conference call.

A myth: Hello VR. Hope we didn't trouble you at work with our invitation.

V.R: Hi all! A myth, I am working from home today. So, no issues at all. Hello Ms. Leyla,, it's my pleasure to see you here. Hope you had a good day, woman.

Leyla: My apologies, but I don't think I know you. Never did I see you on the blog.

Kamakhya: Leyla....LMAO! He is Vikrant, Leyla! V.R stands for Vikrant Rao :P

V.R: Ms. Leyla! That's fine. Apologies accepted.

Leyla: Thanks!

V.R : Leyla, I hope everything is fine today. You sound dull.

Amyth: Yeah, she is.

Leyla: Just like that! I am reading some stuff simultaneously, so please pardon my late replies.

Amyth: Vikrant join us on voice chat.

V.R: Here I join the brigade bro!

V.R joins voice chat.

Leyla switched on her speakers to listen to this 'mystery man'. Vikrant was on speaker and said, "Hi folks. This is Vikrant here. How have you all been?" His voice was deep and husky, very manly. Leyla felt quite strange. It felt as if she had known this voice for years or may be for many lifetimes...this feeling was just so different ...

She liked the quality of his voice and imagined the personality he would have to match with the voice. She imagined a tall, dusky and a broad silhouette of this man.

Kamakhya replied to him, "Vicky! Woaaah! We finally get to hear you!" and giggled in a way that indicated that she was interested in Vikrant. No wonder. Vikrant's replies on the blog were so outlandish that he had become popular among fellow members. But Kamakhya's giggle made Leyla fearful of being replaced by her rival. She anxiously connected herself to the voice chat and shrugged her mood swings aside.

"So here I am friends...:) Hi A myth. Your coffee idea worked for me. Thanks! Hi Mr. Rao. Apologies for not greeting you when you connected. I was feeling low at that time. But all you guys on voice chat were having so much fun that I could not resist joining you...ha ha. Talking here makes one feel that he/ she is on air on public demand. ;)"

A myth: Woah Leyla! Now you are here with us in true sense! :P

Kamakhya: Hey Leyla! You have an impressive and authoritative voice! I didn't imagine your voice to be like that!

Leyla: Oh! Is it Kam? I hope it's a compliment. Lol!

Kamakhya: Of course, it is...coz it's not an ordinary girlish voice.

V.R: Kamakhya, Leyla's voice is bold for sure. But her giggle is like a raspberry plum! Sweet ;)

Leyla's face turned red after reading it, she couldn't stop blushing for a while.

Kamakhya: How romantic Vikrant! How I wish to have such a romantic partner for life.

V.R I am honoured, Kam. You will get the one you desire.

Kamakhya: Rao (laughs), this brings a huge smile on my face. HUGS :)

Leyla: Vikrant, you surely know how to win hearts! Don't you?

V.R: Yes dame and I surely know how to curb hearts too!

This statement left Leyla with goosebumps! She was not sure if she took offence or got alert. She murmured, "Hhmmm…" and remained silent after that.

That night Leyla had a disturbed sleep. She dreamt of being chased by a black horrifying monster with a sharp knife to stab her. She was running through the lanes in some old Indian city with mud houses surrounding the lanes at each end. She escaped and ran till she reached a crowded local market with the monster still chasing her. She jumped over a heap of cotton and reached a dead end. She turned around and saw the black monster standing right behind her. The blood in her legs froze in horror as she remained still, waiting for her death. Suddenly, from nowhere, her mother appeared in between. The monster was about to stab her mother when she woke up. Leyla was shivering with fear and sweat dripping from her forehead to her cheeks and nose. She switched on the lights and drank the glass of water kept on the bedside. She instantly realized that it was the same horrifying monster which she had seen as Vikrant's display picture. She was dumbfounded at the impact of this mystery man in her life. She had no clue how he looked, had never met him. Leyla had just heard his voice and read a few lines written by him. Why was he so impactful? What made him stand out from the crowd…

was it his choice of words or his attitude that reflected from his words? He was particular about everything, from his beautiful italic fonts to the colour of his texts. There was something unique about Vikrant. Something which majority of men do not have, leyla was drawn towards him. She wanted to know more about him. Though there was an invisible wall of hesitation in between. He seemed like a man with dark secrets. She decided to scrutinise all the information available on the internet about him. She got up, connected her laptop to the world of web and started searching about VIKRANT RAO. There were 102 links which included his name. She scrolled the page. There was one link of Princeton University where his name was mentioned and a blurred passport size photo was posted among the five toppers of software engineer batch of 2010. He was also ranked as the best student of 2010 by Intelligent System Groups, Texas.

Leyla flipped a few more links and found his profile on a social networking site. The profile picture here was different from the one which Vikrant used for Beauty Incarnate. She found two of his photographs after searching his profile. She clicked on one, and as it was uploading, she was surprised to see the way her heart was pumping and racing fast. She was curious to unleash the black monster now. And his photo was now wide open on her screen,

The man in the photo had broad chest, was tall and fairer than she had imagined. He didn't have a beautiful face but had an impressive personality. His eyes were inexpressive, bland, tired and cold. He was smiling for formality. He had thin shiny hair. He was wearing a crisp white shirt with a well-fitted pair of blue denims. Leyla didn't find him attractive enough to fall for his looks instantly. He was reasonable in looks, but Leyla expected unique looks, matching with his unique vocabulary and voice! She had no clue if she was disappointed at the way he looked or was amused to find that he looked like a normal human being and nothing close to a black monster! She had mixed feelings about him.

The next day, she was going through the rack of management books in her college library when she saw Avi standing in front of her. At first, her gaze was fixed on his beautiful face. She couldn't react for a while, but collected herself and greeted him with a smile. It had been some time since they had spoken to each other. Avi was not a regular visitor in the library otherwise. His presence in the library indicated that he missed Leyla dearly. Leyla observed him closely and admired his looks. He was fairer than Leyla, tall and fit. He was impeccably dressed, as always, and wore her favourite cologne. She felt guilty of comparing his looks with Vikrant in her subconscious. Prejudices on pretext of outer beauty didn't go along with her core values. She shrugged the thought and asked Avi if he would like to join her for some coffee.

They were sitting in the cafeteria near the glass wall. Avi was talking about last night's party. At the beginning, Leyla tried to be attentive and listen to him, but in a few minutes, she realised that she was bored with this silly conversation. The next moment, she snapped at Avi unintentionally, "We have met after so many days Avi. I expect you to talk something about us, for god's sake!" Before she could complete, Avi interrupted and requested her not to spoil the spirit of the day. Leyla also realised that she was being unfair with Avi. How could she stop him from enjoying the things which he liked in his life! Leyla quickly apologized and contemplated the reason for her behaviour with Avi. She realized that the naked truth behind her anger was the feeling of not being as lucky as him, with respect to both family and circumstances. He could afford to be carefree, while she was haunted by the complicated relationships with her family. Anger thrived inside Leyla. Her cowardice haunted her.

Avi took her hands in his and asked, "Why do you overthink, Leyla? Why you don't lead a normal, easygoing life? We are not super humans, we are not here to change the world. We are common people, Leyla! This life is so short to worry so much!"

Leyla replied, "Avi, it's not that simple. Recently I got acquainted with a guy who is accomplished, polished and proficient. I might not be able to change the world, but I would at least want to live the best version of us, Avi. I expect you to think with a little depth now."

Avi got irritated with Leyla's repeated nagging and he retaliated. "Enough Leyla! I don't want to hear a word from you now. You are one mentally unstable woman. And who is this guy you just mentioned? I am sure you are under his influence! Tell me, are you meeting him? Tell me what is cooking?"

Leyla blew off at his suspicion. "Are you are blaming me? You won't ever get the message, but would rather talk bull crap! Holy shit! I have not even seen him, for god's sake! For your information, I just know him through the blog which I moderate. But no, you would charge me of betrayal. You know why, not because I would ever cheat on you, but because you don't trust yourself, because you know you are not good enough for me. You know you can't contain me inside yourself. Because you know I deserve something more, much more!" Leyla was yelling at him. She instantly regretted what she had said, but now it was too late to undo anything. Avi was shocked, hurt and angry. He stood up and pushed the chair with such force that almost everyone in the vicinity noticed the tiff. He left immediately, leaving Leyla embarrassed and teary-eyed.

She kept tossing and turning in bed that night. Leyla was angry on Avi because he was not what she was seeking in her life partner. He had not seen the downside of life so far. He couldn't match the depth of her thought process because life had been fair to him so far. But why was she penalizing him for being fortunate and not exposed to the darker side of life as compared to her.

She turned on the light, switched the laptop on and signed in to the blog. While she was checking feedback emails with suggestions and complaints from the community members, a message window popped up on her screen. It was from Vikrant, "Hello Ms Leyla, it's nice to see you at this hour."

Leyla: Hello Mr. Rao, nice to see you too. You must be in office!"

Vikrant: Yes Leyla. I just took a fifteen-minute coffee break. Caffeine rush is important for my productivity, you see!

Leyla: So, you are a coffee lover?

Vikrant: I am a coffee addict, dame.

Leyla: I like tea more :)

Vikrant: How has your day been so far?

Leyla: It was okay! Nothing worth mentioning.

Vikrant: Leyla! What do you want to become?

Leyla: Never thought of it! Will finish my studies and probably marry and settle with two kids or pick a job to pass time till I get married. :)

Vikrant: Why do I find you contradicting?

Leyla: Contradiction of what sort?

Vikrant: Leyla, I remember when I joined Beauty Incarnate, it was a gloomy, mundane community with 20 odd members who hardly used to communicate. But after three months, when I came back from vacation, it had a whopping 300 people and most of them were active. This community was alive in its glory! You know why?

Leyla: No! Why?

Vikrant: Because you were made the administrator.

Leyla: How does it matter who the moderator is?

Vikrant: It matters, Leyla! You introduced member interviews. Everybody felt like a celebrity in their own way. You introduced various contests to encourage people to participate. Leyla, you ran the show. You make them laugh, you give them a sense of belonging in that community. You have created an entire association of hundreds of mortals who interact daily. That too when nobody is paying you to do this.

Leyla: These things sound so positive, Vikrant! I am humbled. Thanks. But where did you find the contradiction?

Vikrant: These are the traits of an entrepreneur or a business executive at the top level in an organization. You are a leader. You give hope to people. But when you talk to me in person, you seem sad. Someone who has no dreams, no ambitions. Looks like something is bothering you.

Leyla: Mr. Rao, I wonder why you would say so.

Vikrant: I just know it! That's all. I could see sadness everywhere, from your voice to your texts every damn where! Do you remember my first reply to you about life? After reading that, didn't you feel that I know you already?

Leyla: Yes! I felt so.

Vikrant: Do you think that was a universal reply? No Leyla, that was a reply that you were seeking. That answer was meant for you alone.

Leyla: How do you listen to the words which I do not say, Vikrant? While there are people who live with me all the time and yet do not understand my spoken words!

Vikrant: That's me, dame. I have nothing more to say on that. Now if you could please share the reasons for this vacuum in your life.

Leyla: But you are a stranger, and I cannot find a reason to trust you. Though I can't deny the fact that I feel like talking to you for hours and tell you things I've never told anyone.

Vikrant: Then tell me. You can't trust me, but do you have any option? Risk it, Leyla. You will either have answers or not! You have nothing to lose. But you might gain your life back.

Leyla: I can't afford to be hurt again.

Vikrant: How can I cause you hurt? I am just a voice. I would either show you a direction or will fade away, just the way I came. There is no physical proximity which we share, Leyla. Think! How will I ever cause you hurt?

Leyla: What if I fall in love? You know, you are too good at winning hearts!

Vikrant: Chances are that you will. But then I am replaceable, Leyla. Somebody or something more intense will eventually replace me. Give me six months of your life and I will change it. Surrender to me. Simply confide and you will be a different person.

Leyla: But why do you want to do it for me? Why are you interested in my life? Why should I not be afraid of your proposal? What will you get from doing this?

Vikrant: I am studying psychology as a hobby course, though I am a software engineer by profession. You are my subject, Leyla. In this process, we both will learn something. I will go deeper in my subject and you will get clarity in your life. We both have nothing to lose.

Leyla: You are strange.

Vikrant: I am Le Diablo!

Leyla: But I am only a human being. Why should I enter in your world?

Vikrant: Because I am Le Diablo for the world, not for you. I am exactly what this world deserves out of me. And you are a doll. And I am not asking you to enter into my world, rather I am entering yours to understand how you feel, what you think, how you live. I will be living with you Leyla, day and night. To understand your life and to swiftly remove the barriers in your life, as and when they will appear. So that finally you blossom into a lady that the world would respect; rather than being a girl who is being treated like an object of entertainment.

Leyla: If you are not Le Diablo for me, then what are you for me? And how can you live with me day and night?

Vikrant: Technology! We will be constantly in touch with each other on internet. You will mail me details of how your day is going from college, whenever you will have access to the internet, and once you return home, you will log on to voice chat. And the answer to your first question is that I will be your mentor for six months. Your master! After that I might be replaced or I might be whatever you choose me to be for you. A friend, an acquaintance or a person whom you secretly confide in, or even nothing!

Leyla: What if I chose to be your lover after six months?

Vikrant: I am already in love, Leyla! I can't be your lover in this lifetime. She is in LA. Our marriage looks difficult, but I won't give up on her. We meet every month. Either she flies to meet me or I fly to meet her.

Leyla: Then why should I risk my emotions? I have so much to lose if I fall for you.

Vikrant: Chances are that you will fall for me. But you will not be hurt. That's my word to you. Leyla, you are not the first one whom I will mentor. I have been a mentor before. And all these people love me now, but their love is of a different kind. It's platonic in nature.

Leyla: What if I fall in love as a lover?

Vikrant: Let me take care of that part!

Leyla: Why are you so intimidating Vikrant?

Vikrant: That's me! You think about my proposal and come back to me tomorrow. If you agree, I will be available from 7 p.m. onwards. Come on voice. If you want to say no, leave me a note offline. I will have no hard feelings. We will always share this good rapport.

I know today's conversation is too much for you to absorb. Now I think you must go to bed and relax. You didn't take rest since you came home.

Leyla: Sure. It has been a long day indeed. Good night, Vikrant.

Vikrant: Just remember one thing, if you know how to play with strings to make music on your guitar, then do not teach the trick to everyone. Choose your people very carefully.

Leyla: I did not get you.

Vikrant: I am your special music. Do not divulge me to anyone. This world is an ugly place. Do not tell everyone that you have a mentor. If at all you share, pick them carefully.

Leyla: Sure Vikrant. Now you go home. Take care.

Vikrant: Don't bother about me, Leyla. I am not used to being taken care of. Ta Ta!

Leyla: Bye…

Vikrant: Leyla, I know I am leaving you with many doubts and fears. But I don't want to say anything anymore. It will confuse you further and leave you exhausted. Please spend some time in solitude and you will feel better.

Leyla: Sure. See you tomorrow.

That night Leyla had a weird dream. She saw herself in the middle of a broad highway, all alone. The sky was covered with dark clouds and thundering bolts. She was scared and running on the road to seek refuge at a safe place. Suddenly, Leyla saw one grey old dilapidated building. She had no option but to enter it. It was chaotic inside. Many middle-aged women were sitting in groups and talking to each other. They took a momentary pause to look at Leyla questioningly and continued with their chat soon after that. She passed through the hall amidst the ladies to reach the exit door. As she stepped out of hall, she landed on a veranda with a huge iron gate. It was chained with iron shackles and a huge lock. She banged the gate in fear. This place was weird and the women in the hall were making her uncomfortable with their cunning looks.

She screamed for help, but all in vain. She finally gave up and covered her face with her hands in despair. Suddenly, she heard Vikrant's voice, "Dare you ever give up, Leyla. I am right here". She looked up curiously, but saw an old man in a gate keeper's uniform. He held a large key in his hands. She could not recognize him. She was staring at him blankly while he opened the huge gate wide and gestured at her to step out of the building. She was still looking at him while stepping out of the gate. Just then dark clouds floated away and a beautiful shining sun rose in the sky, along with a rainbow and vivid flowers on the ground. She was mesmerized by the beauty of nature. She wanted to thank the old watchman for his help. She looked back at the gate, but could no longer see the man. The building which stood erect a few seconds ago had crumbled down in front of her. Her heart was racing fast as she woke up and found herself murmuring, "Vicky... Vicky.... where have you gone?" She was startled with the series of dreams she had after each conversation with Vikrant. She went to the balcony outside and sat on the bean bag placed near the plants and beautiful fragrant flowers. It was cold outside. As she gasped, she exhaled a misty breath each time. It was serene and calm. She was missing a companion. But it was not Avi anymore. She exhaled her breath on the glass window, and scribbled "Vicky" on the misty glass. She blankly stared at her scribble till dawn.

Leyla woke up and found herself lying on the bean bag. It was a bright sunny morning. Her neck was aching because of the wrong sleeping posture. She felt lethargic too, but she had to rush to reach college on time. When she stepped inside her bedroom, Leyla's eyes got stuck at the wall clock. It was 11 a.m. already and she had missed two lectures by then. She decided to take an off and rest at home. The conversation with Vikrant last night was too heavy to absorb for Leyla. She was feeling unusual and awkward about Vikrant's proposal. But then she interpreted the dream last night and thought that Vikrant is the only hope she has in life. She was missing Vikrant. But at the same time, she wanted to escape him completely.

She logged on to messenger and went to the kitchen to make a coleslaw sandwich and some coffee for breakfast. When she returned to her room, she found a pop-up message from Vikrant: "Good morning, dame! How are you online at this hour?".

Leyla: Good morning, Vikrant. I took the day off today! You are in office?"

Vikrant: Yes darls. I just had my evening tea. Will leave for home in sometime.

Leyla: I woke up late and had a little headache too. But it is almost night in the US. Why are you in office so late?

Vikrant: I see! Is it the effect of yesterday's conversation? Well, I have a deadline to meet. Working hard, you see.

Leyla: You can say that!

Vikrant: Come on voice, Leyla. I have a meeting in 30 minutes. I can talk to you from my cabin till then.

Leyla wanted to avoid this discussion but as Vikrant brought the topic again, Leyla could not help but tell him about the dream she saw last night. Vikrant was listening patiently as she described the series of dreams she had seen after each conversation they had had. Vikrant told her that she must not misinterpret her dreams and listen to her conscience without any external influences. Vikrant had to cut short the conversation because of his meeting and asked her to meet after two hours, once he wrapped up his work.

Leyla had more questions before she could decide and respond to Vikrant's proposal. Hence, she was eagerly waiting for Vikrant to be back. During these two hours, she tried reading, cooking and gardening, but the anxiety inside her did not let her concentrate anywhere. She left everything and went for a short nap. After a while, she heard the message tone on the system. Leyla jumped out of bed to reply. She could not afford Vikrant going offline thinking that she was unavailable.

Vikrant: Hi. There?

Leyla: Yes. I am all here.

Vikrant: Wow! that was quick! Your name showed 'idle' since last two hours. I had very little hope to catch you.

Leyla: Yes! I was not using the laptop. Did some cooking followed with some reading.

Vikrant: Nice! So, what did you have for lunch?

Leyla: Yet to have lunch. I cooked shrimps with some Jasmine rice.

Vikrant: I am drooling! Slurppppppp!!

Leyla: Do you cook?

Vikrant: Yes, I do. But nothing can beat my aunt connoisseur gourmet in cooking home food.

Leyla: You stay alone or with your aunt?

Vikrant: Now I stay alone since I have started working. Earlier I used to visit my aunt's place on weekends. I was crazy for food cooked by her. I still am, but I live far now.

Leyla: What about your mother? I am sure she must be a superb cook for a foodie like you.

Vikrant: She was the ultimate cook!

Leyla: Was????

Vikrant: She died of heart attack when I was seven years old.

Leyla: Ohhh! I am sorry to hear that, Vikrant. I can't even imagine your pain and loss.

Vikrant: I never lost her, Leyla. She lives in my heart.

Leyla: Who took care of you during your growing years then?

Vikrant: My mom left me and my younger brother with our dad. And he brought us a step bitch!

Leyla: Is she not good?

Vikrant: I hate her with a passion. She is the ugliest piece of shit. Sorry for my words, but I can't use better words for her just to be nice to you.

Leyla: I understand Vikrant. Do not feel awkward. You have step siblings too?

Vikrant: Nopes. She could never conceive. That's the answer to my prayers ;)

Leyla: But you could have prayed to god to give her sense. Rather than praying to keep her away from world's best feeling. It must have been sad for her too!

Vikrant: Leyla, you are an angel. But I am LE DIABLE. It's good that she could never carry. Otherwise I would have killed them.

Leyla: What??? Can you ever kill anyone?

Vikrant: Yes. For self-defense.

Leyla: Vikrant!

Vikrant: I hear, dame. I hear what you don't say. I know you don't like to see my devil side.

Leyla: Yes Vikrant. You are so well read and wise. Why not forget and forgive?

Vikrant: Dame, you are beautiful. This world is not. You are a rare possession in this world.

Leyla: Vikrant! Why did you choose me of all the people in our blog to help? I am sure most of them would be facing some turmoil.

Vikrant: That's because you are special, Leyla. They are not!

Leyla: But you have not spent exclusive time with me to say that I am more special to you than others.

Vikrant: Leyla, read again! And carefully please.

Leyla: I think I read carefully.

Vikrant: I said *you are special*. I never said that you are special to *me*. You are special to the world. I see you as a unique gift to this world, wrapped in a beautiful red satin. You are so pious and undiscovered.

Leyla: No Vikrant. I am no more a pious girl wrapped in a satin. I have been torn and injured. I have been wasted now.

Vikrant: Leyla, you are an angel. You cannot be wasted! I see your pain. I cannot feel it but I want to understand it. I want to understand your heart, Leyla.

Leyla: Vikrant, it's very embarrassing for me to share.

Vikrant: Why Leyla? Do u think you were at fault?

Leyla: Not at all! I am the victim of trust!

Vikrant: Then stand tall in your life and never be ashamed of things you have been a victim of! Who did what to you, Leyla?

Leyla: Molestation. For years. Years and years. Time and again till I reached the age and courage to raise my voice against it.

Vikrant: That's painful.

Leyla: I don't know what is more painful. The molestation or not being heard and trusted.

Vikrant: Did he happen to….

Leyla: No. But sometimes, broken trust is far more painful than a ruptured hymen.

Vikrant: I understand, Leyla. I am sorry to have asked you this.

Leyla: I was born and brought up in Delhi. I hope now you can understand why I am pursuing my grads from Mumbai, away from my family.

Vikrant: I see. I think he is a part of your family.

Leyla: You are right. I have trust issues. I hate my dad for not responding to my hints. I hate my mom for not being protective enough and I hate my brother for not being considerate! The only person who acted on it was my boyfriend, Avi. He was straightforward and warned him.

Vikrant: Ohh! You are seeing someone?

Leyla: Yes! I love him a lot.

Vikrant: What about him?

Leyla: He loves me more than I love him.

Vikrant: I am sorry to hear of your pain, Leyla. I can understand how you must be feeling every time you would see that man. Or should I even call him a man? I doubt. He is a monster.

Leyla: More than that man, what makes my life depressing is the bitterness I have for my own family and loved ones.

Vikrant: Family is the first world a child knows and when they fail to stand tall and righteous, it breaks a child's tender heart. No matter how much I try to understand your pain, I can never feel it enough, Leyla. I am sorry for you have to go through this all alone, but I will help you come out of it. I promise.

Leyla: I loved my family, Vikrant. But this incident has changed all the equations in relationships. It's a lonely world out here.

Vikrant: What about Avi? Is his love not sufficient?

Leyla: I can't relate to him anymore and he can't tolerate me, I guess! He is a happy go lucky man. He can't relate to my sadness. He is unable to be an empath. I won't blame him. He is not mature enough to handle it.

Vikrant: Leyla, if you have problems in your relationship, you must face them. The biggest problem these days is that people are extremists. They simply pack up and find another partner. And the clichéd reason they give is, "it's not working anymore". Darls, relationships are like trees. Initially you need to water the seed regularly, they demand attention and time, but once they blossom, they provide you shade in all the situations of life!

Leyla: Vikrant…how I wish I could tell Avi this. But I guess it's too late now. We hardly communicate these days. And I know I have developed bipolar disorder. I have become a tough woman to handle.

Vikrant: I don't know who you are, Leyla. You are just a voice. But you seem too familiar. Maybe we share a connection from our past life. I don't know. But I can feel you.

Leyla: I wish we could meet once. Just want to feel your embrace. All I want is one hug and you would understand all my pain and suffering.

Vikrant: I feel your emotions, darls. I will ensure that we meet at least once in this lifetime. And take my words Leyla, that day will be the most memorable day of your life. I will share with you which even your husband can't share. I will make you live that day to the fullest. You will touch life Leyla… that day you will breathe life.

Leyla: You are taking me to another world. Don't give me false hopes. I might take them too seriously.

Vikrant: I am a man of my word, darls. I won't ever promise you a life with me. But I will snatch a day of your life and make it into a day you will remember all your life. I am a man you would never forget to have met.

Avi's final exit

Leyla and Vikrant had been talking to each other for long uninterrupted hours for almost three months. Leyla's emotional dependency on Vikrant had increased beyond a point of return. Leyla had totally surrendered to Vikrant and confided in him for almost every aspect of life. Her family dynamics, her choice of dresses, her career, her friends and her diet, everything was being governed by Vikrant, despite the physical distance. Vikrant was totally dominating Leyla and she was happy being submissive. She saw a mentor in Vikrant. And Vikrant often said, "You are my only family." Leyla's world revolved around Vikrant and she was seeing life through Vikrant's eyes, taking decisions through his wisdom, and knowing facts through his knowledge. A rare relationship was taking shape. There was no physical proximity, yet they both were closer than the closest. They were spending days and nights together, hours and hours with each other despite ever meeting each other in person. Leyla had many nights of heart-filled laughs with Vikrant, many nights of silent tears rolling down her cheeks while she shared her sorrows with him. Vikrant was filling-in all her emotions and slowly she recovered from the hollowness of relations in her family and her troubled relationship with Avi.

Leyla was waiting for Vikrant to come online. It was the first time that Vikrant was not online on time. If he had a social commitment to meet, he would text Leyla during the day about the change in the timing of his availability. His absence was making Leyla worried about his well-being.

Leyla's heart was pumping fast with anxiety. What could possibly have happened to Vikrant? Suddenly Vikrant's message popped up. "Hi."

Leyla: Vikrant??? Where were you?

Vikrant: Hey! What's wrong? That's not how you welcome me!

Leyla: You have never been so late without information. I was so worried about you. I had a thousand wrong thoughts crossing my mind.

Vikrant: Darls, don't panic. There is no need for that. My apologies for I was not able to inform you because that was a random engagement.

Leyla: Ok. But where did you go?

Vikrant: Miss Leyla, I am promoted, darling. Congratulate me! Now I am a senior software engineer. That's why couldn't come earlier. Had to take my colleagues out for drinks.

Leyla: Wow! That's an amazing news! Heartiest congratulations to you, Vikrant! :)

Vikrant: I feel like dancing. Will you dance with me and celebrate this moment?

Leyla: There is no physical proximity between us, Vikrant. How on earth is that possible?

Vikrant: Oh Leyla! Stop talking logics here. You know we can dance on the astral plane. Just close your eyes. Meditate and focus inside your mind and keep your body relaxed. Think about the most romantic music and you would feel it playing, think about me and I will be dancing with you. Put your head phones on, Leyla. I want to hear you dancing.

Leyla: But Vikrant, the other day you were talking about switching over to another offer?

Vikrant: Shut up and dance, you lovely bitch! No more questions for now.

It was the first time that Vikrant had talked to Leyla this way. He was opening up to her. This was the very first display of his closeness and emotions towards Leyla in these three months. This sudden honesty from Vikrant had flooded Leyla's heart with emotions. She felt loved. She closed her eyes and began to dance with him. She could feel a gush of energy in her body. She was shivering with desire. She could feel his arms around her waist. She could feel his body against hers, his breath close to hers. This feeling was consuming her senses. She wanted to be lost in this beautiful world of illusion. She began to feel complete with this feeling, with the intensity of her passion for Vikrant. She began to mature as a lady. She could feel heaviness in her bosoms, the desire was taking over her, swiftly. Vikrant heard her deep breath and said, "Doll, you are the most special to me, you are my only family." His words brought tears to Leyla's eyes and she whispered, half asleep, "May I sleep in your arms, only for tonight?"

"Always my dear… you are always in my arms," replied Vikrant.

Leyla's phone was continuously ringing. It woke her up from her deep and relaxed sleep. She looked at the clock and realized it was 8:00 a.m. She should be leaving from home by this time. As she rushed towards her phone, she realized that she had head phones around her neck and the memory of last night came back rushing to her. She shrugged off the feeling and hurriedly reached out to her phone. It was Avi's call. She suddenly felt guilty for what had happened last night. She picked the call, "Hello".

Avi sounded worried and anxious. "Where the hell are you, Leyla? You answered my fifth call!!! Couldn't you hear your phone ringing?"

Leyla replied in her heavy morning voice, "Good morning Avi, I don't know… I was sleeping and woke up with your call only."

Avi tried to calm his voice and said, "I thought I'll pick you up from your home for college. I am already waiting near your house. Aren't you late for college? I was worried… you have been missing your first lectures during the last couple of months. So today I made it a point to pick you up on time."

"Thank you for coming, Avi, but I will take time to get ready. You should go. I will reach in some time".

"No Leyla, I won't mind getting late today. I am waiting for you in the car only. Be quick."

His repeated insisting irritated Leyla but she shrugged her agitation aside so that she could start with the day peacefully. She rushed to get ready and joined Avi in his car.

Both of them were searching for words to strike a conversation. Suddenly Avi popped out an odd question in this odd situation.

"You still talking to that guy you mentioned to me a couple of months back?"

Leyla was taken aback with his question. She was already feeling guilty for the night before and now this direct probing by Avi was making her anxious. Her mouth dried up as she tried to answer. She coughed and hesitatingly said, "Yes".

Avi clenched his face and sarcastically asked, "Is he the reason for your new utmost punctual avatar?"

Leyla's heart skipped a beat. She got frightened with Avi's question. She answered in a fearful and low voice, "I speak to him and he is like a mentor who helps me understand life better. That is all to it."

Avi responded with a smirk, "Really? Does it take an entire night to explain what life is?"

Leyla felt a great jolt on her head and revolted, "How could you say that Avi?" She almost screamed at him.

Avi laughed in disgust and replied, "I know you Leyla. And I know you have changed. I know the reason for this change. Are you talking to him all the time or not?" Avi's tone was hard, questioning and piercing. Leyla could feel her blood freezing. If what had happened last night wouldn't not have happened, she could have easily taken charge of the situation. She knew that Avi had no right to ask her about who she was talking to and for how long. Their relationship was a failure and both of them had to accept it as soon as possible. But it was her own guilt that was consuming her.

Despite what was going on in her mind and the anxiety, she mustered up courage and responded, "Avi, he is my mentor who has taught me how to think, question, seek answers. Even if I speak to him, I am only growing as an individual in the entire process. He is a true human being, just a well-wisher who wants the best for me."

Avi snapped at Leyla,"Really? And who are we, Leyla? Are we not your well-wishers? Your mom, your dad and I. Do we not wish the best for you? Has that stranger influenced you so much that you forget to speak with your own dad? Is this what he is teaching you? Tell me. Leyla! Do you have any idea that your dad calls me to know how you are because you hardly pick his calls and talk to him."

Leyla yelled at Avi, "You are talking about my father? *You* of all the people! You know the reason for the strained relationship that I share with him. You know how many nights I've spent feeling insecure in my own house! You know why I moved out. You know how I was molested in my own courtyard and how nobody heard me or paid heed to the pain and humiliation I went through. What should I talk to him for? For keeping his status, community, and image above my happiness?"

Avi retaliated, "What's your reason for not taking my calls?"

Leyla wanted to fire at him for leaving her emotionally empty, for not looking beyond her physical beauty and understanding her heart. He never believed in her dreams and had often ridiculed them! But she remained mum, starring at Avi in anger and disappointment at his inability to understand her.

Avi repeated his question in a harsh voice, "Answer me, Leyla! Is he the only one who is teaching you things? Have I not taken interest in your education and growth? Did I not research the best colleges for you? Has your father not supported you, your education and comforts?"

Leyla smirked and replied, "Yes Avi, all of you have tried to teach me things, but not in the way I wanted to learn. You all forced your ways on me for your convenience. No one ever tried to dig deeper into my soul. That is what Vikrant has done for me."

Leyla had mentioned Vikrant's name to Avi for the first time. Avi applied the car breaks so hard that the sudden jolt became inevitable. Leyla looked at Avi in shock. He said, "Get down from my car right now, you bitch!"

His words felt like a tight slap on Leyla's face. She was staring at Avi with shock and disgust. She asked, "Did you just say that Avi?"

"Yes Leyla. Please get down. I can't even bear your sight these days. You are not my Leyla anymore. You belong to someone else. You say he is teaching you, you are growing. Bullshit! You are losing Leyla. You are lost. Now you think only what that jerk wants you to think. You are poisoned. You are totally poisoned. That bastard, that son of a bitch has poisoned you against me that all you can see in me are faults. Go Leyla! Get lost from my life. I am done and over with you. My Leyla is dead. This is some bitch who has taken over Leyla's body."

Leyla winced. She was aghast and fell on the back of her seat. She felt ashamed of herself for loving this man ever. All she wanted to tell Avi was if Vikrant had ever talked about her family and Avi, it was an attempt to keep her positive towards them. He had taught her to strengthen the relationships around her. But she didn't owe Avi an explanation, especially after listening to such abuses for Vikrant, the man who was her idol. She recollected herself and her belongings before she was pushed out of car in hatred by Avi. As she made her way out of the car, she banged the door on his face. She couldn't believe all of it had actually happened to her. She was bursting into tears, drowning into the pool of pain and disgust. She came back running to her house and kept crying till she fell asleep, hurt and hungry. Her sleep was broken by her phone ringing. It was Vikrant. Leyla was taken by surprise because Vikrant has called her on her phone for the first time. Though they had exchanged numbers, Vikrant had asked her not to call him until there was an emergency. They had never called each other.

She picked his call, "Vikrant! Is everything okay?"

Vikrant replied, "Yes doll, just called to know if you are okay. I just had a creepy feeling that you aren't."

Leyla was overwhelmed with this soul connection between them. She couldn't control her emotions and started weeping, "No I am not fine, Vikrant. But I am sure I will be."

Vikrant asked, "Have you eaten anything since morning? My hunch says that you are hungry?"

Leyla said, "No Vikrant. How do u know?"

Vikrant said sweetly, "I knew. Baby, listen to me. I can't explain how I get to know things. But just trust me when I say that I am very close to you. I can feel you sweetheart and I got an unexplained drop of tear in my eye. I understood my doll's heart has just been broken. Sweetie, I am in office right now, won't be able to speak to you for long. Just follow my instructions. Go get up and eat something first, and then tell me what has happened over an email. I am worried about you here. Okay? I must rush back to work. Remember that *you are inducted in me. You are mine.* Bye!"

Vikrant's quest

Leyla was waiting for Vikrant to come online while looking outside the window. The night was beautiful. A full moon adorned the sky. Leyla was silently watching a dog who had curled into a lump. He stretched, shook himself and circled before lying on the ground. Leyla was amused and thumped the window with her hand to get the dog's attention. He looked at her for a moment and yawned. She smiled and repeated the same. This time he rolled and rubbed his back and neck and ignored the sound. Leyla was engrossed in this little play when the phone rang.

"Vikrant! I was waiting for you." She excitingly answered her phone.

"Hey! What are you doing, big woman?" Vikrant asked.

"Well, I was wondering that you helped me in a billion ways, but did I help you in your quest for knowing more about human psychology? You wanted to go deeper in your subject. Am I helpful to you in any way or am I just selfishly taking your help?" Leyla asked.

"You want to know?" Vikrant counter-questioned.

"Yes! Of course!" Leyla was quick to reply.

"Come on skype, Leyla. I want to see you." He spoke in an ordering tone.

"Skype!" Leyla exclaimed.

"Yes. I won't come on video, but I want to read out something to you. That will clear all your doubts. I want to see your expressions. Please." Vikrant explained.

"Really! Ok. Let me login." Leyla signed into her Skype account.

Leyla appeared on video call. Vikrant took a deep breath, as she appeared on his screen. She wasn't doing anything. She just stood there, leaning on her room window and smiling. He could see her unmade hair falling all over her shoulders. She had a sculpted figure. Her arched eyebrows and sweeping eyelashes were mesmerising. It was a delight to see her flowing hair and sweet lips while the delicate moonlight fell on her face. For a moment, time had seized for Vikrant. He wanted to capture this moment into his memory, forever. He was swept under the spell of Leyla's beauty. She could not understand his silence anymore and spoke in curiosity, "Vikrant, are you there? Can you see me?"

"Oh yes doll! I was just a little overwhelmed looking at you."

"Why?"

"Most of the time we seize the moment in our cameras, but sometimes the moment seizes us. We feel more alive than ever before. And when such moments occur, something in us changes permanently."

"Vikrant…"

"I know you Leyla! I have known you since ages." Vikrant could barely manage to speak and had a glass of water to get hold of himself.

Leyla could feel Vikrant's state of mind but could not really understand what he meant. She was curious to listen to what he wanted to read out. She insisted him to read.

"Leyla, a few days back I was sitting at a cafe and penned something about you. I had no intention to share it with you, but since you doubted your contribution in my life, I am reading out a few lines from it." Vikrant explained and started reading from his diary.

"Individual, the term, as I coin for this person, remains quite relative in my mindset about her. I say this because I know how different and unique she stands, away from her ethos and biological bonds. This I realise when she talks to me as often as possible, whenever time lies at our disposal.

"Life to me, as it sits settled in my view, is the equation that encompasses reason and the law of causality towards my spiritual attainment of knowledge. She comes as a wonderful addition that can never be ignored. She has knowingly or unknowingly contributed to the share of my mortal life. My pen doesn't stop while describing her. Now that my thoughts streak across even in the most disturbing and difficult ambience around me, my focus on her seems undisturbed.

"Circumstances and situations cannot be denied a casual participation in this process of our bonding. As I try to help her discover her uniqueness against all odds and normalcy that stand, faced eye to eye, I find it quite odd as to how and why her circumstances have been forced to the hostile platforms that she doesn't deserve. I must accept that her portrayal of circumstances and experiences, ranging from her thoughts in every dimension that I share with her, convinces me to think that she is not normal and banal amidst such souls.

"Why should she succumb to situations that force her to become something better and gain a quality rather than forsaking an aspiration? It remains a puzzle to me. I have decided that I shall strive for her and pull her out. She is vivacious and enthusiastic when she comes running to me every evening to share her feelings with me. This very essence can never be captured or compared to the happiness one feels when a child with honest and true innocence comes trolling towards them. I admit that she loves me for what I am and what I exhibit. I feel important when she shares with me her descriptions and portrayals about herself, her binding situations. I find myself in appreciation when I see her dance to her own tunes, even in the direst of circumstances, especially when it comes to me.

"She wants me to feel her and I understand her. As a result, today, she lives inside me and I live inside her. There are a plethora of emotions and feelings that rush from my embodiment of her. My feelings are too pure to be infiltrated by adverse circumstances.

"The knowledge that I gain from her fuels my research about humans and helps me look for my own unique entity. She is worth much more love than what her biological caretakers shower on her. She is such a beautiful life form that fascinates me each and every minute of the time that I spend with her. I promise myself that I shall never give up on her and embody in her a sense of greatness. This strength will give her a reason to be what she wants to be. Her desires fly in space through her imaginations. She is a surprise gift wrapped in so many different emotions. I adore the way she is skeptical of her own self and never inhibits herself from sharing anything from me.

"My universe shifts to a different dimension every evening when she shares her experiences in her own ways; she finds an answer and reason in my shade. She deserves to have a better understanding of life that I harbour inside of me and I will share that with her. I find a great deal of beauty in the way she takes an effort to understand me and my understanding of the world. My heart will always adore her as a princess with a golden crown. She owns the unclaimed place that resides in my soul.

"Should a good force hear at all, then it should understand and fulfill my demand for a greater life for her. This beautiful embodiment of emotional delicacy deserves greater understanding and reciprocation. I want her to be the architect of her destiny. I can hear her loud cry for help, which other people fail to hear.

"She in my belief would be a great, honourable descendant who will lay the foundation of evolutionary and spiritual development and ascend it to the higher level. In my mind, I call her 'A neo-modern Indian female'.

"Unconsciously, she has supported me through the period when I was at a loss of answers to who I am and what I want from life and the people who I want to include in my life. Her timing to enter my life is impeccable. She helped me hold my own character and built it further, with hope and reasoning. This encourages me to shoulder the responsibility and to be the wizard wielding mentor. She will be a priceless asset in my jewel box. I would caption her as a mortal reaching out to the stars, like an angel!'

"Vikrant!" Vikrant could see that Leyla's deep eyes were wet with tears.

"I know you don't have words Leyla, but believe me, your eyes, profound with emotions, just spoke to me. Every tear drop from your sparkling eyes would be engraved as a priceless gift to me on the leaf of my heart and will stay with me till I am alive. I am indebted, Leyla. Indebted to your tears." Vikrant could no longer hold his emotions and opened his heart out.

"Vikrant, I want to hug you. I want to feel the warmth of your embrace." Leyla said in gratitude.

"Me too, doll! I want to hold you physically, emotionally and spiritually, with all desires aside. I want to spend moments of pure serenity with you." Vikrant reciprocated Leyla's intimate confessions with his own.

They knew that their love for each other was platonic; they had highest regards for each other and had placed each other inside the deepest corner of their hearts. Yet, the pain of being unable to feel each other was becoming too much for them to endure at that moment. They could no longer hold the conversation and left each other incomplete, with an insatiable thirst for more.

A myth's apprehensions

Leyla was sipping her coffee while checking Beauty Incarnates' progress. The blog was a part of her routine now. People would write grievances, suggestions and feedback. She would reply to each of them and would execute some suggestions, if needed. Leyla and A myth were joint administrators of the blog.

This blog and its three thousand members were like an extended friend circle for Leyla. A myth's real name was Amit Trivedi. He had adopted the name 'A myth' to be used for the blog. He was studying mass communication in Mumbai and was Leyla's close confidant. They were administering the blog together since the last one year and raised the number of members from a meagre 120 to a whopping 3000. For the first time, an ad agency had approached them for flashing a two-minute advertisement on their website. Leyla was excited on reading this.

She pinged A myth.

Leyla: Hi! Did you see the message from Broccoli, the ad agency?

A myth: Yes indeed! We are getting famous! (:D)

Leila: Yes! What should we reply to them?

A myth: Leave it! It's a hoax. In fact, delete it and report spam.

Leila: Really?

A myth: Yes. I already did my research on that.

Leila: Ok! Hey, did you see the response on poetry competition? Overwhelming, yeah?

A myth: Yes. I wanted to discuss something about announcing the winners too. Who do you think we should announce and when?

Leila: Yes. We should announce that tonight. Kamakhya's poem has been voted by most members. But, I found more substance in Vikrant's poem. What do you suggest?

A myth: Leyla, we can't be biased. The number of votes and popularity should be the parameter to declare the winner. Vikrant writes extraordinarily well. We all know that. But he fails to connect with ordinary people. We are a blog for ordinary people, Leyla. We are not running a contest for poets.

Leila: Will you reject perfection for the ordinary?

A myth: Leyla, the objective here is to run the blog. The objective is to connect with masses and keep them happy. Please refrain yourself from diversion.

Leila: You did not answer my question!

A myth: Yes Leyla! I would! Because the rule of the contest was crystal clear. It is the number of votes and comments which will define popularity and the most popular poet will be announced the winner. We never asked for perfection. We asked for maximum participation. Kamakhya's simple and well-articulated poem has attracted more people. Vikrant's poem could engage only a few exceptionally serious readers.

Leila: Ok. Then let's announce Kamakhya as the winner. However, I am not impressed!

Life is nothing but a picture
It's sorrow's and fun's mixture

We miss someone like a heartbeat
It chokes me with a bitter sweet

Irony is , nothing can be expressed
A lot remains hidden and unsaid

But a ray of sunshine gives us hope
It is like cleaning off dirt with soap

As a beggar has nothing to choose
But it does lead to mind's abuse

No matter what destiny has in store
I don't care if I have to suffer the lore

I will still remain reckless, I won't fear
Will never let anyone see my tears

I will die with my heart wounded
Even if the life that remains is hounded

U have come as a flicker of flame
Nothing is left for me to claim

I won't let you go ever
A cloud or sunshine doesn't matter

Life is nothing but a strange maze
Don't get lost in the stupid haze

No one can steal you from here
Even if I have the worldly fear

Keep moving in the winds like a cloud
Never ever think twice or doubt

My existence will be like air
Never seen but you can't spare

Love is an emotion which goes into the drain
So never let your emotions go in vain.

Read this A myth! You want to announce her as the winner?

A myth: Yes. I am. Seriously! What's wrong with you Leyla?

Leyla: Why?

A myth: Leyla, you have changed during the last couple of months. You know even I admire Vikrant. But that does not let him overpower me or dictate my decisions. Why are you trying to do that here?

Leyla: I am just asking you to announce him as winner because he deserves it. Does that imply that I am trying to be something to him or I am biased?

A myth: Leyla! It's not about this poem only. Please read your own poem now.

When I saw life from a human's perspective, devoid of holistic picture, I found tragedy…

When I saw life from a god's perspective, absolute and whole, I found comedy…

When I saw life from a devil's perspective, devoid of intentions, I found parody…

Look at your life not like a participant, but as a spectator, my friend. You will find melody!

Do you think it's your style of writing? Leyla, you have expressed your emotions. You are best at writing on relationships and love stories. Since when did you start including devils in your writing?

Leyla: I was trying something new, A myth!

A myth: Yes indeed! But all I could find was Vikrant's reflection in your words. There is nothing new. It's a mimic of his writing style. At least I felt so. I am your well-wisher Leyla. Don't lose your original self. He is great. Let him be. Don't try to match his greatness with yours. You are unique in your own way.

Leyla: I don't agree with you. However, I do respect your opinion. Good night!

Leyla was disappointed. A myth was a well-wisher. Somewhere in her heart, she knew that he was right. She was not sure though. Why would she try to be like Vikrant? Why did people who know her, perceive it like that? First it was Avi and now A myth. She discounted Avi's allegations as jealousy but A myth had made her think now. His purpose was achieved. She now realised that A myth wanted her to think about this. But she had an instant justification in her head. After Avi's exit from her life, Vikrant was the only influence she had. He was mentoring her. He was creating a strong impression on her. So, the merging of identities was natural.

Avi and Leyla never spoke with each other after their last spat. However, they passed each other like strangers inside the university premises. Neither of them spoke to the other. Leyla was able to overcome her painful break-up with Avi only because of Vikrant. He had become the centre of her life. She was immersed in his love and affection. Leyla's break-up with Avi was inevitable, but not acceptable to her. The break-up left behind a void. It had made Leyla bitter and clueless about life. She missed her classes, and barely managed minimum attendance to appear for the exams. However, she passed her exams with decent grades only because Vikrant had helped her with the subjects she was weak at. Leyla was lonely, sad and vengeful the all the males in her life. Avi's indifference and immature approach towards her feelings had broken her spirit. Love was a long-gone thing now. She was deeply attached to Vikrant, but she was sure that she couldn't fall in love with him. She had loved Avi with all her heart and pure intent. Now she had lost him.

Leyla finished college and went home for vacation. She utilized this break to figure out what should she pursue next, a job or further studies.

Her father came home from work and greeted Leyla." Hi Leyla! Good evening!"

"Good evening, dad! How was your day?"

"It was good, Leyla. So, what have you decided to do next?"

"I am still exploring, dad. A job, hopefully!"

"I happened to meet Avi today. He is also at home for vacation."

Leyla's heartbeat dropped at once. But she tried to look calm and didn't ask further questions about Avi. She was afraid that her father will get the hint if she changed the topic. Her father continued without noticing anything, as usual.

"He is leaving for the US to pursue PG in international business management. His flight is on 23rd September, in just 14 days from now. You never told me that he had plans for USA?"

"Dad, I had no clue. We don't talk much now."

"Why Leyla Ji?"

"Just like that."

She switched off her system and walked away without bothering to see if her dad had anything else to say. She locked herself in the washroom and burst into tears. She was shocked. Avi had decided to leave the country and didn't even feel the need to tell her once? "How big is his ego? Was it love at all? Could he leave me and go forever?" she spoke to herself.

She felt like calling him and crying aloud in anger. Leyla wanted to ask him why he didn't understand her love for him. She had loved him. Why did he hate Vikrant? She wanted to tell him that Vikrant will not exist at all if Avi confesses his love for Leyla. Only if he said he respected her, that he would try his best to understand her inside out. She felt like explaining to him that she was incomplete without him... that she had loved him to an extent where she couldn't see him bending low at any point in life. Leyla couldn't see him being irresponsible or not able to follow the right path. But this didn't mean she did not love him. She wanted to enlighten herself spiritually, wanted to know what life is and give a true purpose to her life. If Avi could not help her find it, Vikrant had. Why did Avi doubt her soul-searching as a love affair? They might be attached because of Vikrant's deep understanding of Leyla's true nature, her soul, but does that justify Avi maligning her character? Leyla's thoughts made her feel intense and restless, but she could not muster the courage to call Avi and say that she loved him! It was too late now. Will he ever come back? Will Avi ever understand her love for him? She felt disappointed because she had very little hope of him coming back.

That day, Leyla was anxious and felt directionless in life. She waited for Vikrant and flooded him with questions as he appeared online.

"What's my aim, Vikrant? What's my purpose in life? Why do I find all my relations inhuman? Why can't I connect with them?"

Vikrant: Leyla, I don't know what is wrong with you today, but I can see that you're hurt. Why?

Leyla: Tell me Vikrant! Tell me why I am born in this world?

Vikrant: You are born to achieve your desires and you would achieve them, no matter what. You will throw materialism away and bring spiritualism into the picture. Your real desire is the desire to achieve and be a better human being in this lifetime. And for that, you will abide by the laws of your current world and move ahead. In some ways, you have already moved ahead, but you might have left something behind for which you may be sent here again. That's why you are in a place where you feel people are immature or inhuman or have lost the essence of being human. It's not that they are inhuman, they are yet to evolve to match with your definition of a human being, mature and self-aware.

Leyla: But Vikrant, what am I here to achieve? Can love be a part of my accomplishments?

Vikrant: The real relationship is spun with many strands. It takes your desires, your soul and your life form with its laws and your true nature to materialize them. In the end, you either quit or win. If you win, the completion of those desires goes with you and remain with you in the next series of lives.

Accomplish love once Leyla. And you will have it forever, in every birth.

Leyla: I do not even know what my desire is, love or self-discovery?

Vikrant: Your desire is to have a composite relationship. That's what you yearn for! For that, you will be challenged. You will be put through situations to make you understand that perfect relationships do not come easy to anyone. You have to struggle for some and sacrifice for others. Some will make you suffer and for some, the experience of separation will help you value them and preserve them inside your heart, forever. It's simple. If you want to buy a car, then you need to earn money for fuel and for its maintenance. Such are desires and relationships. They require maintenance for they are for you to keep with you forever, since your desires reach beyond death.

Leyla: Why do we have desires? Desire means materialism, isn't it? A spiritual or religious person won't have any desire since that's where contentment comes from!

Vikrant: Desires are means to follow, but not the goal. You are an earthling right now, so the laws of earth apply to you. To move forward from here, you should move in context of what binds you to your soul and what binds you to yourself. Religion is a path to follow real liberation, which lies not in religion, but within ourselves.

Spirituality is the from within and religion is a mere fundamental. Your soul believes only in one thing and that's the yearning to reach the source of energy. Your desires are independent of your lifestyle. You have made certain choices and that's where your desires lay hidden. What's material is your way to abide to the laws of earth where you need to run after money to materialise your desires. Your soul moves forward only when your desires are not forsaken or forgotten, whatever you might be put through to realise or how costly your desires might be."

Leyla: Does it apply to humans only? What about animals? Why don't we have a manual to live so that we know what choices to make?

Vikrant: "Not only humans, every living being has its own ends to meet. The constraints we face underline the value of things which are needed to make ends meet. Humans created these constraints themselves. For example, money was introduced by humans. No life form gets a manual to teach them how to lead life. If we had a manual for life, there would be no diversity. Each one of us will lead life in a similar manner. The Hindu Sanatana dharma can be called a manual, but can't always be practised in modern context. How could one follow the rules or principles which humans make but do not conform with? Each one of us is supposed to follow their own desires which bring them happiness and solace. One should aim at becoming a better human being during this lifetime.

Leyla: But there should be some common ideology to live by.

Vikrant: Ideologies are developed by humans. It's important for everyone to reach their epitome from fundamentals. No ideology, howsoever detailed, can be applicable to every aspect of life. Understanding life by seeking answers from within is possible once the fundamentals come are rightly absorbed. These fundamentals from the knowledge of philosophy, psychology and religion. It is essential to understand human nature before making decisions in life. There are multiple ways of doing that. Each human being interprets learnings differently and have a different motive behind their actions. Again, if the ideologies across human beings are the same, there would be no diversity in life.

Listen to what I say, doll. You are not going to settle for any entry level, officer-grade job. You will do an MBA. I have thought about it and sure about the fact that you are far more capable to be wasted like this. Please get the application forms of the PG colleges on priority, and apply. We will then start preparing for the entrance exam.

Leyla: But Vikrant, I am not sure if I can focus on further studies. Avi has taken a part of me with him. I am not myself anymore. I am shattered into bits and pieces. I can't comprehend a paragraph correctly and you want me to study a whole course for two years?"

Vikrant: You must overcome the pain caused by Avi. He was not destined to have you in his life. You are made for greater things. He could've never contain you. His dreams and aspirations are too small, Leyla. You are special. You are going to fly.

Leyla: His dreams are still alive, Vikrant. No matter how small they are. My dreams are dead. I don't understand how you think that I am special. I have not moved out of the house in months. I have stopped socializing. I don't want to do anything. I lack direction, Vikrant.

Vikrant: You are looking at your break-up through a magnifying glass, Leyla. Don't do this. It's not as big a deal as you are making it. He was not destined for you.

Leyla: How can you say that Vikrant? He left because I never told him how much I love him and how I am suffocating without him. Vikrant, I miss his smile. I miss his craziness for me. I miss him with every second of my life. I don't think I will be able to make it without him. Allow me to speak to him. Allow me to go back to him.

Vikrant: Do you trust my judgement and decisions for you?

Leyla: Of course, I do!

Vikrant: Then listen to me and do as I say. He never loved you. Abuse can never be a part of love. Even if I forget the way he treated you that day in the car and on other such occasions, I can never forget that he has been selfish and left you alone in this state to go abroad and make his own career. Can't he understand your mental state after what you have been through and the issues in your family? Leyla, I can never leave my woman like this. If he was suspicious of you, he should have spoken to me. He should have confronted you maturely. He does not deserve you.

Leyla: Does 'being worthy' matter in love? I love him, isn't that enough?

Vikrant: Bring me any other guy and I will allow you to marry him. Not this man, Leyla. He doesn't love you. You are blinded by emotions. I have made my point. No more discussions on this.

Leyla was contemplating Vikrant's words of wisdom. She understood one thing, if she wanted to go far in her quest to seek her soul, she had to forsake her love. Because nor would Avi approve of her journey, neither will he ever understand the gist of it! But sacrificing her love in this lifetime was a painful one. She might never feel complete after letting Avi go.

Life is meaningless without love. She had no clue about where will life take her. Leyla was led by her yearnings and what if Avi mocks at her dreams. It was a battle between her dreams and her love. Both were equally precious to her. Leaving one for the other was a tough choice to make. Choosing love meant forgetting her own self and changing into a person whom Avi would connect with. If she decided to chase her dreams, she was bound to feel incomplete and loveless for the rest of her life! Was there a possibility of both going hand in hand in life? Leyla was doubtful. She needed a life manual for that for she was scared about the consequences of her decision. Vikrant would never influence her in taking any decision. He was a mentor, not a dictator. But in this decision, he was upfront and unshakable. The day Avi and Leyla drove the final nail in the coffin, Vikrant was hurt with Avi's behaviour. He had said, "That's not love Leyla. That's not love. Choose any man in your life once you start accomplishing your dreams, but not him, Leyla. Abuse can never be a part of love."

Leyla felt torn into parts. She hated Avi for not being the one and still making her fall in love with him. She felt helpless. But true love cannot have conditions. Who did she hate more? Did she direct it to Avi or to herself for being unable to forsake her own definitions of love and life for Avi. She never wanted to answer this question. Leyla kept running between looking within herself and hating him pointlessly.

"Leyla, we have reached home." Maya parked the car in front of Maya's apartment.

Shahan was engrossed in her story. He did not realise that the journey had passed and they were home. He was still intrigued and wanted to hear it till the end. However, he gauged the paucity of time and asked Leyla to promise him that one day, she should write her story and let the entire world read about this beautiful and platonic love story between Leyla and Vikrant. For the first time, Leyla could see her purpose in life. She imagined herself in a book café near the seashore, writing her book. She imagined tourists dropping in and sharing their stories with her. Leyla imagined that she was writing their stories and sharing them with the world through her books. And in the end, she also pictured Vikrant bringing her the best aromatic coffee, while she felt weary after typing on her typewriter for hours. Leyla always wanted to own a book café, but for the first time, she could clearly envision her dream. She was overwhelmed.

Aman's insight

Aman wrapped up the monthly review meeting. It was Saturday today, which was officially a holiday. But Aman wanted to utilise the first Saturday to plan coming month's revenue targets. Everyone desperately waited for Aman to call it a day. Most of them had their weekend planned with friends, however, Aman proposed a team lunch at a nearby restaurant. Half-heartedly, people nodded and joined him for lunch.

They went to an Indian restaurant and ordered Indian cuisine to suit everyone. The restaurant had an economy lunch menu and an average ambience.

Aman asked everyone to share their future plans with him. While most of them had vague plans and some of them had promotions in mind, Maya shared her interest in opening a fashion store. Leyla never knew that Maya wanted to be a fashionista! It came to her as a surprise. Aman asked Leyla about her plans. She kept silent for a few moments as she had no clear answer like Maya. She was not sure if she wanted to stay in the corporate world. She thought hard for a moment and said, “A writer, maybe.” Aman smirked and said, “Madam, I have seen many writers struggling to afford a pack of bread! That’s so unimpressive.”

“When did I say I will work for money? That’s so rude, Mr. Malik. Why should people be judged on such choices?” Leyla was baffled.

“Are you going to be financially dependent on your parents for your whole life? Or you plan to marry off a rich man? So that he slogs and you write.” He smirked again.

“That’s mean! I have never thought of marrying a rich man, ever!” Leyla spoke with agitation.

“Then? What are your plans to feed yourself? How will you pay your medical bills?” Aman asked her, with his usual sarcastic smile on the face.

“I want to open a café library. Some books, a canvas, a guitar. People can have coffee and indulge in their hobbies at the same time,” she said.

She had always thought about this dream, but had never said it aloud to anyone so far. That was the kind of life she had always wished for herself. Secluded and peaceful place where she could meet travellers and explorers from diverse backgrounds. She could translate their life experiences into short stories after meeting them at the café. Leyla planned to open it at a place which was frequented by tourists, maybe near a beach. But she never worked on her dreams as her father was not rich like Maya’s father. He was an IAS officer. Respected, but not rich.

Aman smiled while looking at her and said, “You are a dreamer, Leyla. But the world is for real. I wish you all the best for your dream.”

Leyla knew what he was trying to say. She understood that there was a cost to her dreams. And she had no idea about how long would it take her to reach there.

Aman interrupted her again, “By the way, what will you name your café? I hope I will get some coffee for free over there, once a while!” He giggled.

Leyla smiled back and replied, “I haven’t thought about the name yet. But yes, you can have coffee for free as long as you agree to entertain us.”

“But I don’t know anything besides investment banking!” He winked at Leyla.

“How regrettable! You have hardly experienced life.” Leyla spoke gently. She wanted to make him realise what he was missing, yet she felt inappropriate to speak more on the subject.

“So most probably, Maya and I would come in our Bentley and Merc respectively to have a free coffee at your café. We would give you a chance to drive our luxury cars as we understand that you run a small cafeteria and cannot afford such luxuries.” He laughed and teased Leyla.

Leyla laughed but reserved her comment. She did not mind Aman mocking her dreams. Avi had mocked her poetry and her dreams like that, always. She used to be upset then. But with time, she had learnt that people will mock her dreams because it reflected the struggle within themselves.

Lunch arrived and everyone rushed to grab a bite and leave as early as possible to enjoy what was left of their weekend.

While people were bidding good-byes, Aman walked up to Leyla and said, “I never intended to make fun of your dream. But I have learnt the value and power of money the hard way. I wish life was as simple as your dreams are. Don't get me wrong, but first be financially secure. I would be the happiest person to visit your dream café. But you need to earn that investment first and save some money as back-up, if at all your idea does not work for some reason."

"Yes. I understand and I respect your concern." Leyla smiled.

"Everyone dreams, Leyla, but not with same conviction and belief. Those who dream while sleeping, wake up to find a different reality. But the dreamers of the day are worth my attention. Be a daydreamer Leyla, dream with your eyes open and realise them. Life usually has different plans than we have for ourselves. Your plans should be stronger and your actions, persistent." Aman said to her warmly and left.

Leyla could relate with Aman's perspective. She took a cab and kept thinking about his last sentence. Life seldom gives you what you want. Life has a plan which is different than yours. She went into the memory lane and thought how her life had changed during last couple of years, especially after she enrolled for MBA.

MBA – flashback

Leyla made it to one of the good MBA colleges in Delhi. Vikrant had been with her all this while. He taught her day and night on voice chat and made her crack her entrance examination. First few days were difficult for her as she had stepped out of her shell which gave her a long refuge, especially after the break-up with Avi. She was under depression. She had issues in striking a conversation with new people and was mostly silent and lost. Leyla was unable to mingle with her classmates. They were chirpy and bubbling with youthful energies. They loved shopping, watching movies, hanging out in groups at the latest hangout zones. Leyla felt outdated and thought she'd outgrown them. She had no interest in doing things which people of her age enjoyed doing. Avi's memories haunted her day and night. The more she realised her love for him, the more she hated his indifference. She got to hear about him from her family members and often wondered how easy it was for him to move on while Leyla was still struggling to accept it. As time passed, the memories turned her love into hatred and bitterness.

The saying 'out of sight, out of mind' was proved wrong in Leyla's case. The geographical distance was making it more intense for her. Leyla was stuck in this one-sided relationship and drifted further away from her family. She used to leave home early morning and would return late in the evening. She would speak to Vikrant once she was back and would be locked in the room till dawn. Her parents thought she was working very hard, which she was, but they had no clue about Vikrant's presence in her life. They were not capable to understand her pain, agony or her relationship with Vikrant. He was her only family now. They shared sorrows, laughter, tears, dreams, aspirations and desires. He helped her in making presentations, taught her subjects and at times, did her assignments too. But whenever she brought up Avi's topic, he got annoyed. His answer and decision did not change. There were moments when Leyla almost gave up and requested Vikrant to allow her to quit MBA. But he held her tight and helped her through. He understood the pain of loss of love, but never believed that Avi had loved her. He remained stern and cold. Leyla was through her first year of MBA. All the men who had romantic interest in her knew that she was seeing someone. If anyone approached her, Leyla did not refrain herself from taking Vikrant's name and nip the romance in the bud. Vikrant called Leyla. He seemed happy and excited. Leyla asked him the reason. He requested her to come online urgently as he had break some news to her. Leyla was in the middle of her class but could not resist the urge to log in. As she did, Vikrant's message flashed on her screen," Hey, there! I am so excited. I have been selected for Carnival Inc. I had my final interview and cracked it. The best part is, they are giving me a new on-site project in India as team leader! I will control a team of twenty people there. Woohooooo! I am coming to India, Leyla. Coming back to my homeland, coming to you, darling."

Leyla: What!!! Wow! Wow! Wow! You are coming to India! Wow!

Vikrant: The project is based in Pune, but the head office is in Gurgaon. I will be flying to Gurgaon first for project designing and then shuttle between Pune and Gurgaon after six months. You know, getting this kind of an opportunity within just one year is unbelievable.

Leyla: Wow, that's amazing news, Vikrant! Wish I could hug you right away. I am sure you have worked very hard for this, Vicky. I am so happy! I feel like dancing here, in middle of my class.

Vikrant: Oh no! Control yourself, Leyla. I am sorry, I should have waited for your day to be over, but could not resist. I want to know how far is your place from Gurgaon?

Leyla: It is a twenty minutes' drive, depending on traffic.

Vikrant: Leyla, do you remember I mentioned about the love of my life during our early conversations? When you asked me what if you chose me as a lover after six months and I had told you I am already in love and can't be yours in this lifetime.

Leyla: Yes, I do remember.

Leyla never brought up this topic again because she always felt that she should respect Vikrant's privacy. Incidentally, she had almost forgotten that this lady existed in his life. A sudden mention by him made her feel insecure and afraid of losing Vikrant.

Vikrant: Darling, Cyndi was in LA. She hails from a rich family and her father would never approve a middle-class Indian man to marry his daughter. But yesterday, she gave me a surprise.

Cindy and her father were planning to fly tonight to meet me. She has finally convinced her father. Wow! Wow! Wow! I can't believe it. Wish me luck, Leyla.

Leyla: All the best. Nice, isn't it?

Vikrant: What kind of a reaction is this Leyla? That's not how you express yourself when I am happy!

Leyla: How do you expect me to react, Vikrant? This is normal. Moreover, I do not know Cindy. How do I react for someone's happiness when I don't know the person?

Vikrant: Leyla, just read what you are saying. It's a bitter reaction. You should be happy for me, not for the unknown.

Leyla: Oh yes, I am happy for you, Vikrant. You finally have the love of your life. My professor has been looking at me for a while now, Vikrant. He is suspecting that I am not doing the assignment. Do let me know about your meeting tomorrow. All the best. Bye!

Vikrant: Lol wait. You are not happy! Maybe it's the loss of your own love that you can't see me having it!

Leyla: What an ugly allegation, Vikrant! I won't take it! Bye!

She signed off.

None of them texted each other during the day. Leyla came home with a heavy heart and remorse. She skipped her dinner and did not speak to anyone at home. She went to bed with teary eyes but couldn't sleep that night. Finally, Leyla decided to break the ice and texted Vikrant.

Vikrant,

I am sorry for today. I am happy for you, don't take me wrong. I do not intend to have an affair with you, but yes, there is a feeling that you are mine. With this news, I suddenly felt that I lost you. Yes, you may say all these feelings are uncalled for, when everything was clear since the beginning. But Vikrant, was it just me who is responsible for such feelings for you? Aren't you equally responsible, more responsible, in fact?

Vikrant replied:
Isn't it obvious that it's me who inducted the feelings inside you? But ultimately, you are the carrier of these feelings. There are so many people out there dying in hospitals, with no chance of survival, yet the doctors plant a hope in them, a desire and love for a life which they can still dream of, despite being on their death bed and hoping that a miracle will save them.

It is not me who wanted to be happy and live life on her own terms. It was you, Leyla. I just revived your WILL again.

You will know why my love is different.

Leyla was still unsatisfied with his reply and countered him:

You were my mentor, Vikrant. With time, my feelings changed. I would again say that forgive me if I am wrong, that I am not the only one responsible for intensifying my feelings. Why did you say I am inducted in you?

Vikrant replied calmly:

I expect my relationship with you to be unbound and not defined by a name so that it exists till eternity. The sad part is that you are not the first person I have loved this way and that is the reason I can't belong to you and only you, not in this lifetime. You must forgive me and understand that if in few months' time,

I was able to make such an impression, just imagine five years of such a bond with Cindy and how deep inside my heart she would be.

Leyla:
Vikrant, nobody has loved me the way you have. Nobody felt my pain, my happiness, my feelings, the way you did. How will I be able to manage without you now? The relationship we share is an illusion, but I seem to have taken it for reality!

Vikrant:
While I was deeply involved with you, do you think I thought of you as an illusion? I don't think so, Leyla. I have lived your life with you and that's how I am able to understand you in more ways than one. Nobody ever loved you the way I did because they found a loving servant in you. But for me, she was a special girl, maybe a queen; a woman who would serve herself, will be happy doing what she is best at and knows when to stand for herself, when to sigh and never quit on challenges which life throws at her.

It's not me playing here, but she was mine and that's what I shared with her. Even her husband won't be able to share that with her. If I am a replaceable in someone's life, don't you think I would eventually be replaced by an emotion that is deeper than mine and closer to you. That's why I foster so much love for my subjects, especially when they are mired by circumstances. I lend them my strength to climb back up and shine again. I do not know of any other way to make things work. There is a difference in our core values which cannot be overlooked, Leyla.

This is why we can't become one. I have poured in my feelings with the words for you, Leyla. It was harmonious, unlike most literary connoisseurs who use language and expression and like the psychic savants who use theory of purpose and problem unemotionally and cause more depression, prove to have alternate solutions that are not convincing…

I am a blend of both. That's why I am and I can't change. The magic of my words is 'one hand and one lung'.

The right hand and lung is my ability to understand people and feel for them when they are weak. Sooner or later, this ability turns into love. I am not saying that I didn't love you. It's just that I love someone else more and it's hard for me to forget her.

With left hand and left lung, I feel for them as I express emotion with my right hand and right lung. I write for them, understand them and that's how I embrace a person, like you.

Leyla decided to get hold of her life again. She understood that she had no future with Vikrant. Her emotions were as temporary and short-lived as Vikrant in her life. She had to let go of her insecurities and possessiveness for Vikrant. Though Vikrant and Leyla had taken the conversation in their stride, but there was an unseen wall of reluctance between them now. Vikrant was not warm and affectionate as before and had very formal conversations with Leyla. She also hesitated to face him for many days since she felt guilty of either expressing her feelings to him or having felt anything for him at all. The relationship between them grew cold with each passing day, so much so that they wouldn't talk to each other even when they were online. They used to be a part of community conferences, but the communication was restricted to formal greetings, just like strangers; they were avoiding each other. Almost a month had passed. Leyla tried to move away from Vikrant, assuming that he would be engaged to his lady love. Her life was filled with vacuum. She was trying hard to apply Vikrant's teachings in her life, but her loneliness made her feel like an injured bird stuck between hurts caused in the past and uncertainties of the future.

Leyla was looking for jobs and filling registration forms online on various websites when her phone rang. It was Vikrant. Leyla's heart skipped a beat. She had no clue why Vikrant was calling her after all these months. She assumed that he might be calling to invite her to his wedding! She didn't want to be unreasonable this time and decided that she would extend her warm wishes and congratulate him. She took the call and spoke confidently.

"Hi Vikrant! Long time…?" Leyla pretended to be normal, but her heart raced as she spoke to him.

"Hi Leyla! Was missing your chirpy voice in the community conference. You haven't logged in during the last couple of days?" Vikrant's voice was soft, affectionate.

"Does my absence still make a difference to you?" Leyla ended up being sarcastic and unreasonable with Vikrant. She regretted immediately though.

"Leyla, you are inducted in me!" Vikrant spoke softly.

"Vikrant, please don't shower me with these sudden emotions. I am over with it, I guess." Leyla decided to overcome her fear and said, "Anyway, when are the wedding bells ringing?" Vikrant's sudden and unexpected affection had irritated Leyla.

"Ms. Leyla, I thought you would come and ask me about my meeting with her dad next day. We spoke, but you were interested to know if I had dinner? Why didn't you ask me about that meeting which was so crucial to me?" Vikrant raised his voice and darted the question towards Leyla.

"Vikrant, going by the formal communication between both of us, I assumed you are trying to maintain a distance and getting engaged to Cindy." Leyla replied in confusion. She could now sense something was not right with Vikrant all this while.

"Assumptions! I hate assumptions! You assumed all this and reached the conclusion that I am engaged now. However, I needed you, all this while. I couldn't understand why you never asked and started drifting away from me. After that night, you were never mine, Leyla. You didn't behave the way I know you would. The way you come running to me and confide in me. The way you claim me, own me." Vikrant sighed.

"You confessed your feelings for me that day and I understood, but stepped back." Leyla justified her decision to be distanced with him.

"So, you mean you confided in me earlier assuming that we will be together someday?" Vikrant fired at her again.

"Not at all! That was natural and unconditional!" Leyla defended herself.

"Where did natural feelings vanish after I declared my love for Cindy?" Vikrant countered her again.

Leyla had no answer for him. She didn't even attempt because somewhere she knew she was wrong and Vikrant was being genuine. She redirected the conversation and asked him, "What about that meeting with her dad?"

"It didn't work out," Vikrant replied.

"Oh…why?" Leyla was now concerned.

"He had already finalized a guy for Cindy in his mind. He came to LA only to stand tall in the eyes of his daughter. He had a condition which made me back-out and he conveniently put the blame on me, for not marrying her," Vikrant spoke gently.

"What condition?" Leyla asked. She was both concerned and curious.

"He said that there is a multi-millionaire family who want their son to marry Cindy. He is the son of a big business tycoon and loves his daughter very much. Cindy could marry me only if I were ready to move in with her in their mansion, follow their traditions and their lavish way of life. Did I mention that she is not an Indian? She is from Greece," he replied.

"I am sorry to hear this, Vikrant. I had no clue. I am sorry for not being with you during these testing times. I am feeling so small right now." She regretted her childish behaviour.

"But what was Cyndi's stand on this?" She felt sad and wanted to see some hope in his story.

"Well! She feels I should agree and get married first. She can convince her dad later that it'd be better if we live on our own," he replied.

"But she might be right. He has agreed for your marriage. Slowly, she would have made him agree on other things too." Leyla tried to tell him that all was not lost.

"Leyla! I can read between the lines. I know how her father is. I could see his motive behind agreeing for the marriage. He needs an heir for his business. I know Cindy too. She won't be able to see through her father's motives. It was not meant to be, Leyla. I can't and will never be a pawn to somebody else's ambitions," he explained patiently.

"I am sorry, Vikrant!" Leyla apologized again.

"I tried to stay away from you due to your ruthlessness, but I realised there are no coincidences in life. Your relationship failed and mine followed. Maybe this bond is deeper than we thought it is!" Vikrant was now telling her the reason behind calling Leyla.

"Vikrant…"

"Ssshhhh! I don't know what future holds for us, but let's give it an honest try," Vikrant said.

"Vikrant….I …..you….I mean….should we….reconsider?" Leyla was not prepared for this.

"Why are you so stressed about it, Leyla? I didn't ask you to marry me. I said let's give it a shot and see if we are compatible. I understand you have come out of a long indulging relationship and you are emotionally stuck there. You should understand my situation too. We both are emotionally stuck-up. No matter how much we deny, we both need to move on and close those last chapters. We might not find each other compatible for marriage, but can walk a few miles together and move on!"

"Yes, we can, Vikrant. But our cultures and upbringing is totally different." Leyla was being practical.

"That is secondary, Leyla. I am just taking our friendship to the next level which is deeper than the bond we share right now. Let us see if love develops. Till this point, our cultures should not be an issue." Vikrant assured her.

"What if we find ourselves compatible with each other?" Leyla had her doubts.

"Then obviously cultures will never be an issue. Compatibility would mean understanding, trust and respect. If we have it for each other, we will take anything to our stride," Vikrant reassured.

"People from diverse cultures should be together only if they are madly in love! Otherwise, why should they even try?" Leyla could not make much sense out of this sudden situation. She was deeply attached to Vikrant, but a relationship had never crossed her mind. She was not prepared for an unusual relationship.

"Leyla, do you see any man in your life as capable of understanding you the way I understand you?" Vikrant asked her, hoping to convince her for his proposal.

"Not at all!" Leyla replied instantly.

"Then I am sure you won't be able to settle for an éclair after tasting Cadbury Silk." Vikrant laughed notoriously and lightened up the entire conversation.

Leyla felt relieved and blushed but continued asking, "Okay, I won't be able to settle down with anybody else! What about you? Why do you want to be in a relationship with me?"

"You are my only family," Vikrant said confidently.

"But you said there are many students in your life and there is some degree of bonding with each one of them. Then why to choose me as a companion?" Leyla was not yet convinced.

"Because they didn't touch my heart like you did. Your innocence and inquisitive nature blew me off at times. Nevertheless, I love your smile and I missed it, Leyla. I missed you. I felt incomplete without you. My days were dull. I thought it was because of Cyndi. But when I missed you in the community conferences and during the nights which I usually spent with you, I realised it's you I am missing more than her. I am not saying I love you, but you are a part of my present and I want you to be a part of my future too. When you are not there, something inside me goes silent. A part of me keeps looking for you. Are these reasons not enough to tell you I need you?" Vikrant spoke in a gentle and warm tone.

Leyla was silent. She felt loved and developed a sense of belonging for Vikrant. But for her, a relationship was meant for life. This 'no commitment relationship' didn't make sense to her.

She questioned Vikrant again, "What if you see me as part of your future and I don't or vice versa?"

Vikrant answered, "Leyla, let destiny unfold its drama. If it's meant to be, it will be. What will happen in future, will be seen with time. But wherever our destiny takes us, I am sure we both will evolve into better human beings."

Leyla tried to share her insecurities, "Vikrant, I owe you my life. A break-up leads to bitterness, complaints and ill-feelings. And these feelings come as a package if a relationship doesn't work. It has shattered me before. I cannot bear with the pain once again. You are too special for me to lose to a failed relationship. That will be a very costly bargain."

Vikrant replied, "This love which you have for me will never let anything go wrong. If we decide to part ways, I am sure it will be peaceful. What we both share is beyond this puny world of relationships."

Leyla had tears in her eyes. She was still waiting for Avi to come back. It had been two long years. She knew that all her hopes will go in vain. He never tried to reach her all this while. She knew she must move on. She knew that now was the time to decide and bid goodbye to this unending longing for Avi.

Leyla disconnected the call, opened her laptop and answered him via email, in his style.

He looked deep into her eyes
Their souls entwined
Neither the bodies touched nor the lips sealed
Yet their love travelled beyond the seas…Their broken spirits healed.
He often said, "my love, your happiness is my duty."
She felt loved…every word he spoke, glorified her beauty.
They travelled together on hills and in woods
They danced under the moon light and read worldly books.
What on the earth could be more enthralling
Than to see two hearts, one promise and love sprawling.
She looked back into his gaze and her spirit melted
He pulled her close, their chests welted.
Soaked in the love, they remained floated
They wished to be together, forever love-coated.

All this has happened in our dream world so far.
Leyla is waiting for you as she thanks her stars!
With love and tears of joy,
Leyla

The twist (back in present)

"Hi darling! I am with Shahan in GK M block market. Helping him with last minute shopping. And from here will go to VISA office for some paperwork. Are we catching up in the evening for coffee?" Vikrant asked Leyla.

"Vikrant, I am in Noida for a client meeting. Maya is coming back to office from her meeting. I will coordinate with her and get back to you. We need to see if Mr. Malik is in office. Because if he is, then it will be difficult for us to leave early. But how come you are out today? Didn't you have to go to work today?" Leyla asked.

"Oh! I forgot to inform you that Shahan joined me for lunch. He needed some company. I wrapped up my work early today and met him," Vikrant replied.

"I see. You forget to tell me many things these days, since Maya has introduced to Shahan. You are having a lot of dinners and lunches with your new buddy. You forgot your Leyla," she joked.

"Ha-ha! I want my Leyla to work hard and get promoted soon. It's her time to grow in her career. But yes, I will agree that Shahan and I get along well. Ok. You let us know about your plan. See you," Vikrant said.

Before she could disconnect, Shahan snatched Vikrant's phone and said, "Miss Jealous, don't be insecure. I am here only for another fifteen days. Vikrant will be all yours thereafter." Both of them giggled and hung up.

At 7 p.m., the four of them met at a fancy Mexican Restaurant in CP. The ambience was lively. They ordered some Jalapeno Poppers Smoke Fajitas and Chilly Verde with long island iced tea for the ladies and beer for men.

"The Jalapeno Poppers are not Jalapeno Poppers. Where is the cheese filling?" Shahan asked the waiter while he laughed.

"You mean they are not poppers, but robbers," Vikrant joked.

"Yes, they are robbing us! We are paying for no fillings. Hey, let us find out if we are paying for a chef who does not exist, maybe their mopper has cooked our popper!" Shahan continued the joke.

"Shut up guys!" Maya was laughing madly. "Stop it now…it's not that bad."

"I will make sure that she joins you in California. She is my responsibility," Vikrant said while sipping his beer.

"How will you send her to California? It's not funny, Vikrant. Don't over commit." Leyla interrupted.

"Why? Why can't I?" Vikrant questioned in agitation.

"It's not like eloping to another city. There are visa formalities. She needs finance. Moreover, Shahan is going there as a student.

How will he manage a married life? Are you kidding all of us now?" Leyla lost her cool.

"Who said she will go there and get married to him? They will marry each other eventually. I also know she will not get visa without a solid reason and a travel visa won't suffice. I have already planned that. She will prepare for TOEFL. I will help her seek admission in a university based in California," Vikrant spoke firmly.

"But why? She already has an MBA degree and is working in a good firm. What are you saying Vikrant?" Leyla almost yelled at him. Everybody was puzzled with Vikrant's plans but Leyla reacted frivolously. Shahan asked her to keep calm and allow Vikrant to explain what he has in mind.

Vikrant continued, "See, I understand that Shahan is a student there and Maya's parents will push her to get married while she is here in India. You are taking an education loan and as per my understanding, you will take at least three years to settle and take further responsibility in life. So, Maya goes to California to pursue further studies. Her parents will not be able to say no to her. Maya studies in the same city as Shahan, eventually find a job and get married."

"Study what Vicky? She has already done an MBA!" she raised her voice again.

"The MBA degrees from India will not get her a job in California. I know it. And pursuing and MBA again makes no sense. Maya, last time when we spoke at length, you told me that you don't like this job. You did MBA to buy more time from parents and postpone your marriage. I remember you telling me that you wanted to be a fashion consultant," Vikrant continued.

"Yes Vikrant. I always wanted to be a fashion consultant. But how do you think it's possible?" Maya was puzzled.

"I don't know if Leyla ever told you, but I have pursued dual masters in the USA. I am a software engineer by profession and a practicing psychologist, informally. I am not just a preacher, Maya. That is the reason I have students who swear by me. I preach what I practice and I take pride in saying that. After doing an MBA, you have learnt the art of business. A course in fashion consultancy will help you realize your dream of becoming a designer. You can even start with something of your own after that. I did my research and found some amazing universities in California. All you need is a TOEFL score and you'll be eligible to apply," Vikrant explained.

"But if they are premier universities, why will they admit me? I have no background in fashion." Maya seemed unconvinced.

"I have already spoken with an immigration consultant. He said that most of these universities will seek your designs. If they like them, they will conduct a personal interview and then you are in." Vikrant cleared her doubt.

"Designs? But I don't know how to stitch!" Maya retorted.

"Maya, that is what they will teach you. As preliminary level, they want to see how creative you are, how you experiment with colours and the fashion sense you have. So, draw it on paper, write a summary and send it to them!" Vikrant tried to clear Maya's inhibitions.

"But I have no knowledge of materials and fabrics. What will I write in the summary?" Maya asked again.

"I will train you. It's a one-year diploma. And Shahan's is a two-year post-graduation. You still have one year to prepare yourself before going there. Admissions are open for October session next year and we are sitting on 18th January today. We have some time to prepare," Vikrant assured her.

"Okay! And all of this will come with a cost, I am sure. What about finances? Studying abroad should cost a minimum of ten lakh rupees, at least?" Leyla got perturbed at his ludicrous plans.

"That shall be seen later. If her parents are convinced, we will get it funded from them. After all, nobody knows that she is eloping. Otherwise, she will have to prepare hard to get a scholarship," Vikrant replied calmly.

"My parents will never fund me. Neither will they allow me to pursue studies abroad. This is out of question, Vikrant. And Leyla has a valid point. Where will money come from? I will have to elope even for studying there." Maya supported Leyla's concerns.

"Can we think of funds once she has an admission letter from the university? Let's take baby steps and focus on one thing at a time. And if money will be a roadblock, I will take a loan to help you, I promise. You can repay it once you are comfortable." Vikrant was getting irritated with continuous questioning.

Maya smiled with gratitude and said, "Thanks Vikrant. But I will try and work it out on my own. Money should not be an issue. I can sell the solitaires that I wear and get five lakh rupees instantly. For love, this sacrifice is nothing."

"I can request my parents to help me with the rest. They will do it for my happiness, our happiness. They are not against our marriage," Shahan assured.

Leyla's heart pounded fast. She had no idea why but her sixth sense warned her about something fishy. She could not explain it to anyone else. Maya and Shahaan were impressed by Vikrant's plan but she found it to be irksome and unethical. She even tried to explain, "See, I know Maya's parents since childhood. I know it will be next to impossible to convince them. But eloping like this is not right. You guys should not marry without their consent, that too in a different country. One day, they might agree."

"Leyla, it's a do or die situation. Maya's parents had once caught us sitting with me in a restaurant. She confessed that I am her love. You have no idea what happened after that. She was thrashed, her family came to my house, yelled at my parents and accused them of misguiding their daughter. They threatened that they'll report my parents to the police and what not. Maya had a hard time convincing her parents that she won't see my face again. Only on this condition did they agree to let her continue with her MBA!" Shahan explained.

"Oh! You never told me about this, Maya." Leyla was appalled at the revelation.

The flashback had made Maya emotional. She broke down in tears and said, "Who wants to run away from parents? Who would want to break their parents' heart to start a new life? But I have no option. It is a choice that I have to make between my love and my parents."

Leyla realised that nobody would understand her apprehensions. The situation was out of control. Maya was already looking for someone who could help her elope and she had found Vikrant. The plan was final. Nobody sought her advice. She decided not to say anything and nodded with everybody, despite being unconvinced. The only thing she was confident of was Shahan. He was a genuine guy and she knew he would keep Maya happy and comfortable.

Shahan's departure

"I will miss you darling…." Maya could not even complete her sentence and broke down in tears.

"I will miss you too! I am sure Vikrant will help us in getting back together again. It's a matter of a few months baby. I love you so much!" Shahan held her close and consoled her at the airport.

"Mom, dad please take care of her. Please make sure you are in touch with her." Shahan requested his parents.

Shahan's mother came forward and held Maya, "You are a brave girl. You love for Shahan is so deep, Maya, despite the fact that your parents don't approve of this relationship. Come here, doll. We are there for you and you will join him soon."

Shahan's mother was a Christian married to his father who was Muslim. She too had to elope and marry. She could feel Maya's pain. She was supportive and affectionate towards Maya.

Leyla held her back, kept stacking the strands of her hair behind the ears. She was too emotional to say anything.

Leyla was furious at Vikrant for not coming to the airport even after Maya requested. She texted him, "Sometimes I don't understand your decisions. Maya needs us right now. Why didn't you come?"

"Don't be silly, Leyla. I feel awkward at airports, when it is about bidding goodbyes. I get nostalgic. How many times do I need to tell you this?" replied Vikrant.

"And how many times do I need to tell you that this excuse doesn't go well with your personality! Convince me with a better lie!"

"Later! I am busy right now," Vikrant replied.

Leyla was infuriated at Vikrant, at his dismissiveness. Shahan hugged everyone and walked away. Maya kept looking at him till he went out of sight.

Vikrant didn't call Leyla back the entire day. Leyla was seething in anger but she decided to discuss her issue with him. She called him, but he didn't pick her phone. She got worried and texted him, "Keep your anger aside and please tell me if you are okay!"

"I am ok." He replied within a minute.

Leyla was fuming now. She texted, "What have I done to deserve this treatment, Vicky?" She kept on gazing at her screen, waiting for a reply which never came and fell asleep.

Next morning, Leyla called him after she boarded the metro. Vikrant took the call this time. "Yes, tell me?" he said.

"How the hell are you speaking to me Vikrant? Why are you behaving like this?" Leyla spoke, rather loudly.

"See, I have only ten minutes to speak to you. Make sure you don't bother me after the eleventh minute since I am in office." Vikrant was rude and cold.

"Vicky! What have I done?" Leyla gritted her teeth in anger.

"You tried to overrule me. You did not understand me. You tried to command me. You are intolerable, Leyla. I am an adamant guy. Next time you won't instruct me, especially during my conversations with Maya and Shahan." Vikrant retorted in anger.

"But why can't I have my say? We are both equal in this relationship, Vicky!" Leyla fired at him.

"You say whatever you have to when it comes to our personal relationship. If I had followed someone's instructions about how to handle you, you wouldn't be the woman you are today! I am the mentor. I decide what is good and what is not!" Vikrant asserted.

"Okay Vikrant! Though this sounds strange, I am sorry for my lack of understanding. Can I have my old Vicky back now?" Leyla gave up and tried to resolve the issue.

"I will try. Give me some time to come back to normal," Vikrant said.

"Ok, take your time. I love you. Bye." Leyla smiled and disconnected the call.

The issue might have been resolved, but Leyla could not come to terms with Vikrant's behaviour. This was not the same Vikrant she had known all this while, whom she had fallen in love with. She was in office but worked half-heartedly. She didn't go to any client meeting that day and postponed all her appointments. Mr. Malik, the CEO, noticed that something was bothering her. He texted her from his cabin. "Are you okay? You don't seem to be."

"I am fine. It's just a mild headache. Thanks for your concern," replied Leyla.

"Please come to my cabin."

Leyla entered the cabin hesitatingly and greeted Aman. Aman asked, "See, I am almost seven years elder to you, Leyla. Though I might look younger!" He giggled and continued, "I know the world seven years more than you do and I know that it's not a headache but a heartache that's bothering you. Ain't it?" Leyla was feeling odd with Aman being informal with her. During the last three months, Aman has had informal conversations with the team, thrown parties when the team performed well and discussed their individual dreams too. But he had never been this pally with her. She attempted to hide the truth by saying, "Nothing like that, sir. Some personal issues occupying my head have caused the headache."

"What issues? Only if I may know? Is it the usual boyfriend stuff?" grinned Aman.

"Naah. I am thinking about new client acquisitions." Leyla lied.

"Oh, come on Leyla! Don't give me this! You are performing well and cannot have a headache because of this reason. You can choose to tell me the truth or don't say anything at all." Aman said in a gentle yet inquisitive tone.

"Actually, there are other issues too. But I won't be comfortable sharing them. Sorry if that disappoints you." Leyla honestly put forth the truth.

"Leyla, you are not comfortable because you don't trust me. I am not trying to get personal here. I believe we spend more time in office than at home, and office becomes your extended family. Do you know the attrition rate of my team is the lowest?" Aman questioned.

"No. But how do you manage to win people's loyalty?" Leyla asked him.

"Because I believe a true leader is the one who understands his pupils. And you can't help them grow without knowing about their issues, dreams, aspirations and their psychology," Aman explained his reason to ask her issues.

"I agree, sir," Leyla said.

"It's not just about your career here. We all move on in life and will reach a new horizon, which is unknown right now. But this is your launch pad and I am your first boss. I believe in mentoring, not dictating. I would like to shape the professional in you," Aman continued to explain.

"I appreciate that! Your team talks highly about you. Now I know why." She smiled.

"Leyla, I have been working in this industry for seven years now. Many team members who report to me have more years added to their age and work experience. I have been able to gain their respect," Aman said.

"How did you do that, Aman? What's the secret of your success?" Leyla asked.

"Trust! I always base my relationships on trust. This helps me understand them better. The loyal ones are the assets. Ones who break my trust are filtered. Do you know why I am telling you this?" Aman continued with the conversation.

"No…errr… maybe because you are teaching me rules of being successful and effective ways to manage people," Leyla spoke unsurely.

"No! Because I noticed that you have trust issues," Aman said bluntly.

Leyla could not utter a word. Aman had got it right. She felt vulnerable in front of him. She wanted to vanish from there. She pretended to make an important call and excused herself. As she moved out, she was crying uncontrollably. The memories of those dark days, the molestation, her conflicts with her father, her brother's rude remarks, indifference, her break-up with Avi – everything flooded her mind. She needed Vikrant. Vikrant was like a drug who could keep her sane. She walked out of office to avoid bumping into any colleague with her eyes which had reddened and hurt with tears. She called Vikrant and bursted in tears, "Vicky!"

"What happened Leyla? Is everything okay?" Vikrant asked, concerned.

"I am suffocating Vikrant! Those old memories have come to haunt me again. I need you Vikrant." Leyla cried again. She wanted to hug him and ensure that he was still the same Vikrant. The one who she had fallen in love with, deeply, miserably.

"Why are you being so childish, Leyla? Both of us are working right now. How could you lose control over yourself in office?" Vikrant got upset.

"Vikrant! Are you the same person who called me from office when I used to be sad… you would just know, somehow?" Leyla was shocked.

"Leyla! You can't expect me to treat you like that for the rest of your life. I had to pull you out of your pain at that time. Now I need to work hard for our future," Vikrant said.

"But why did you change so suddenly?" Leyla was far from accepting Vikrant in the current avatar.

"You are stretching the conversation unnecessarily, Leyla. This is getting on my nerves now. Maya will meet me in my office in some time. I have to take her to the immigration consultant and submit her TOEFL form. I am in a hurry and need to wrap-up before she reaches." Vikrant dismissed her insecurities.

"Maya? She never told me she is coming to meet you! She was in a client meeting." Leyla was surprised.

"Big deal! Am I not informing you? She had come to Gurgaon for the meeting. So I told her if she could spare two hours to close immigration formalities." Vikrant wanted to disconnect the call.

"No big deal? Really! Sure Vikrant. It has been a bad day for me. Take care. Bye." Leyla disconnected in dejection.

Leyla felt extremely annoyed that Maya didn't have the courtesy to inform her that she was meeting her boyfriend. But she calmed herself down. Vikrant had changed, so did the way he spoke to her. This was not her Vikrant anymore. She felt heartbroken, sad and exhausted and left for the day, informing Aman of her ill-health.

But Leyla was worried now. Inside her heart she knew that something was not right and wanted to find out what that was. She could just hope for things to get better.

Vikrant's you turn

"Cheers! We achieved the first milestone!" Vikrant was celebrating with Leyla and Maya at Bar One cafe in Hauz Khas Village.

"I am so happy Maya! You are one step closer to Shahan now. You have eighty-two percentile in TOEFL. Now that's unbelievable!" Leyla said and hugged Maya.

"Guys, this would have been impossible without your support. Vikrant, the way you have mentored me, who does that? I mean, you just know me as Leyla's friend, that's it." Maya was filled with gratitude.

"It is fine, Maya. I am glad I could be of any help. Real hard work starts now. The designs! TEOFL was cakewalk. But preparing the designs without having any background in fashion will be a challenge. Don't take it lightly at all!" Vikrant warned her.

"Vikrant, do I need to worry when you are there to guide me?" Maya giggled.

"No Maya. You need to put in a lot of hard work. I have applied for a fifteen-day leave from Monday onwards. You should make the most of this time. Take as much of my help as you can." Vikrant informed her.

"Really! Will you be on leave? Wow Vikrant! We will be enjoying the weekends, at least. It's been ages since we spent some quality time together. I don't mind giving away your weekdays to Maya, but please book weekends for me." Leyla chuckled.

"I know, darling! I am so sorry. I am taking a lot of your private time. But wait for just two more months. Let me get admission in a good university and I will not invade your space anymore. Vikrant, I am indebted to you guys for life! Seriously. I know I have hijacked your relationship. But I love Shahan so much that I get totally selfish at times and forget that you guys also have a life." Maya apologized.

"I understand, Maya. You don't need to explain. We are like family. We have a right on each other. I asked what is rightfully mine and saved the weekends for us!" Leyla winked at Maya.

"Ohh, before I forget..." Maya opened her purse and handed over a packet to Vikrant.

"What's this?" Leyla curiously asked Maya.

"I am taking it only because you trust me, Maya. Even if you have slightest doubt, then keep it back. I don't want you to get insecure about it and lose your sleep because you have a lot of hard work to do and I can't manage your insecurities at this moment," Vikrant warned Maya.

"Guys, will anyone tell me what is going on here?" Leyla asked again.

"Leyla, I know you won't approve of it. But we have no intention to hide from you. Look Leyla, it's a costly affair. And I don't want to sell my solitaires as my parents will take my happiness if I will tell them I lost them. I will sell them in America. But right now, I need funds for my tickets and visa. Since Shahan is not here, I can't go and ask money from his parents. I decided to start saving a little money for that and keep it safe with Vikrant. He can take care of how and where to spend the amount."

"Saving money? How? From your salary? Then you can always keep it in your salary account. Why give it to Vikrant?" Leyla enquired.

"No. This money is not a part of the salary. I will need urgent money for paying advance for accommodation there, etc."

"How did you arrange money apart from your salary?" Leyla asked suspiciously.

"Err…I took it from the business payments," Maya hesitatingly answered.

"Business payments?" Leyla was cornering Maya with her questions.

"Vikrant, can you explain to me what is happening here?"

"Well, see, Maya is aware that her father will spend any amount worth 1-2 crores for her marriage, only when she marries a man of his choice. Since this will not happen, she is taking away her share. Maya wants to use that money to go to California. I think she deserves what is rightfully hers. Once she leaves the country, her father will sever all ties with her and declare her brother as the custodian of the entire amount. Maya is taking just three percent and letting-go of ninety-seven percent of her share!" Vikrant explained.

"And you approve of this, Vikrant?" Leyla was aghast at this revelation.

"It's her life, Leyla. She needs to decide how and where to arrange the money. I am just a facilitator. But I find no harm in her claiming what's rightfully hers," replied Vikrant.

"Maya, how will you justify this to your family?" she asked Maya.

"When business payments come, a portion of it is black money. Dad keeps the cash in his safe. I know where the keys are. I just took it away," Maya said.

"Wow! What will happen when he finds out what his daughter has stooped down to?" Leyla asked.

"Well, three lakhs is nothing. He is unlikely to notice. My mom and brother often take money out from it, for shopping and other expenses. Nobody will suspect if three lakhs are missing," Maya assured.

"You are robbing your own house, Maya!" Leyla said. She felt dejected.

"Leyla, I know it's wrong. Vikrant knows that it's ethically wrong too. But do you think I am doing it for a wrong reason? My family does not understand me, or my love. They are the ones who are wrong. I am just trying to help Shahan. Because I can. Do not overthink, Leyla. We have reasoned out everything, philosophically, morally and emotionally. This seems right to me and is the need of the hour. Let it be." Maya tried hard to convince Leyla.

"Whatever. My heart and head both say that it isn't right. Both of you did not consider involving me before making this decision. I can only be a silent spectator at this point of time." Leyla picked up her handbag and left the café in utter disappointment, leaving both of them baffled.

Aman's intimidation

"Hi. Good morning!" Aman greeted Leyla while passing through her cubicle.

"Good morning, sir!"

"Were you able to schedule an appointment with Mr. Raheja? The lead which came to us from the priority team?"

"Yes. He has called me to his office in Greater Kailash, post lunch today."

"Great! He is a big shot, Leyla. Make sure you are well-prepared."

"Well, I was thinking if a senior team member could accompany me. I am not confident to handle this meeting all alone."

"Yes, I agree with you. But the branch manager already has all his meetings lined-up today. Let me see if I can go. Remind me around 1 p.m."

"OK."

Leyla dialled Aman on intercom at 1 p.m. and said, "Hi sir. Will you be able to make it to the meeting with Mr. Raheja?"

"Oh yes. Good you reminded me. Could you please ask the office guy to heat up my lunch? I will quickly grab a bite and leave in fifteen minutes."

"Yes. That sounds good."

"Have you had lunch?"

"I will have it in a bit."

"Come on! Let us have a quick lunch and leave."

"Ok. Sure."

Leyla and Aman had a brief business conversation over lunch. They rushed for thc meeting. Aman headed to the parking area to get his black Honda Accord, while Leyla waited for him near the elevator. Aman picked her up. She sat on the front seat with a little hesitation. The car was lightly fragrant with plush interiors. Aman turned some soft music on the moment he started the engine. Leyla observed Aman put on his Armani sunglasses. It was for the first time that she had noticed him as Aman; not as her boss, but as a fellow colleague. He had always been stylish and well dressed. His choice of brands from sunglasses to perfume, even music, reflected his style. Suddenly Aman asked Leyla, "Do you like music?"

"Yes. And this is one of my favourites!" replied Leyla.

"Mine too! Take this iPod and play whatever you like," Aman said.

"Thanks sir." Leyla took a quick look at the playlist.

"Leyla, can I make a request?"

"Yes. Please." Leyla looked at him.

"Don't call me sir outside office. Call me Aman. In office, we have a culture of salutations, I don't encourage it though. But when you call me 'Sir' outside office, I feel like an aged man." Aman spoke hesitatingly.

"Ok sir, I mean, Aman." Leyla laughed and nodded in agreement.

"That is better."

"Maya and you are childhood friends?" Aman asked.

"Yeah! How do you know?" Leyla answered him in surprise.

"A team-member told me. Anyway, that's not important. What is important is that she is not in the customer meeting right now." Aman looked at Leyla with questioning eyes.

Leyla was stunned. She didn't know how to react. Before she could decide, Aman interjected and said, "And I know you are aware of it."

Leyla's mouth dried up, and she tried to handle the situation.

"Well, no. I think if what you are telling me is true, then I do have a fair idea of her whereabouts." Leyla said. She looked in different directions and adjusted her hair.

"I don't care if he is her boyfriend or brother. In sales, we know people across industries. Maya has been seen clicking pictures in the malls in Gurgaon and drawing pictures in coffee shops with the same man," Aman continued to talk, ignoring Leyla's discomfort.

"No. He is not her boyfriend, but mine." Leyla suddenly said this in jealousy and immediately cursed herself for being so stupid.

"What? Your boyfriend is spending time with her?" He smirked.

"No. Actually, he is not just a boyfriend. Since you know, let me explain. Vikrant, my boyfriend, is wise and responsible. Maya wants to pursue further education in fashion technology from California. He is just helping her realise her dreams and get admission in a top-class university there." Leyla opened up and gave him the required details.

"This sounds so funny! No matter how ethical it may look to you, but she has not been performing at work, Leyla. And I am here to deliver. And I will be able to deliver only if my team is committed and persistent. Maya can't be an exception, simply because company incurs a certain expense on each staff. Each one of us needs to justify that cost. I don't mind people chasing their dreams, but not at the cost of my company. I am telling you all this because I want you to give her an informal warning. She should treat this as her last." Aman's voice turned cold and unsympathetic. He had a stoic expression on his face. Leyla shivered in fear; as if she was the culprit. Aman noticed the piercing atmosphere he had created and suddenly withdrew. He selected country music to ease the atmosphere. "So, you have a boyfriend? And he is very intelligent and helpful. Nice to know, Leyla. There are very few left like him these days."

"Yeah," Leyla was still recovering from the shock.

"What does he do for a living?" grinned Aman.

Leyla replied with pride, "He is a senior software engineer with Carnival Inc."

"Wow! So he is settled, intelligent and helpful!" Aman said, with his face smeared in sarcasm.

"Well, there is more to him. He is spiritual, philosophical, a man of substance, a man of his words, mentor for many, well-read, wise, accommodating, particular, a man with high standards and ideals. I can go on and on and on. In short, he is a perfect human being!" Leyla spoke with great delight.

"Then why aren't you happy Leyla?" he asked.

Leyla was silent for a few seconds. Once again, Aman could see through her. His eyes could see her soul. She could not hide from him. He knew nothing about her and yet knew everything. Everything that Leyla knew and something which even she didn't know. Aman was becoming a mystery now. He has suddenly become more than a boss, but not a friend yet. Who was he? Leyla's intuition said that he had a vital role to play in her life. He was just not a boss, but another missing link to her destiny. There was a question that was unanswered. What role will Aman play? Will it be positive or negative?

Aman gauged Leyla's discomfort and lightened the conversation. "So, what do you generally do on weekends?"

"Well, I try to spend it with Vikrant since we are busy with work on weekdays." Leyla tried to smile but could not hold it for a long time.

"Any hobbies?"

"Yes. I like to write and read. I am an avid reader. How do you spend your weekends?"

"Well, for me, weekend has no definition. I started my career with a salary of fifteen thousand per month, seven years back. Today I take five to ten lakhs per month. Do you think it's possible for me to enjoy the weekends?" smirked Aman.

"Someone in office told me that you usually work till 9 p.m. over the weekends too! I wanted to know the reason for this workaholism?" Leyla tried to indulge in the conversation to ease her anxiety.

"What option do I have?" Aman counter-questioned.

"Family? Wife? Children? No time for them?" Leyla asked.

"I am not married, Leyla. Do I look old enough to be a father? If yes, then I need to give marriage a serious thought." Giggled Aman.

"I just thought a VP would most probably be married." Leyla was embarrassed again.

"Is there a thumb rule for that? I started working at the age of twenty-two and just turned twenty-nine, waiting for the right life partner," Aman said.

"Right partner! Don't tell me that in twenty-nine years of life, you haven't met one?" Leyla retorted.

"Not everyone is as lucky as you are, Miss Leyla! Anyhow, I am not seeking a perfect human being like you are boasting of. I need her to be mature enough to understand me and sensitive enough to love me." Aman blushed as if he just met this woman right there in his thoughts.

"How would you know that you have met one?" Leyla asked.

"I will know. The day I will speak about her to someone, I will have a wide smile on my face and happiness in my heart. I will know that I am the luckiest man in love to have got her. I might not have so many adjectives to define her Leyla, like you do, but I am sure I will have one sentence to say. She will complete me with her simplicity and sincerity. She might not be human personified for me, but will be *love personified*. And I am happy with this much. I don't want her to love me intelligently, but to love me innocently and whole-heartedly." Aman explained to her softly.

Leyla smiled at him and wished him luck. But Aman's description reminded her of Avi. Did he love me whole-heartedly? Did I seek intelligent love? Did I become greedy and asked too much from life? Had I bargained for a poor deal? Had I bargained a heart for a head? Her heart was sinking. Suddenly she was reminded of Avi's smile. His innocence while telling her funny things about his friends and other non-stop stories of parties and hostel days. Him giving her funny names and hugging her like a child hugs her mother. Saving her number with "say" and the way he would laugh like mad and explain "because you keep saying and I keep listening" when Leyla caught her. Clicking cute pictures and printing them to post it on his almirah. Wearing her jeans and flaunting to his friends, "See even our waists sizes are same!" and getting Leyla embarrassed. But the good memories were soon followed by the end and how he brutally abused her, alleged her of having an affair with Vikrant. How he had insulted her, attacked her dignity, character and called her names. How easily he forgot the good times, made no effort to save the relationship, made no effort to read her state of mind, especially after the molestation. He just gave up and opted for a new life. The love in her heart changed into hatred. She was dragged into the memories of her past and was trying hard to come out of it. If the decisions driven by heart are so hurtful, she would rather like to be driven by her head. She was sweating with anxiety. She took a deep breath to come out of her inner conflict.

Aman could notice her discomfort and asked if she was okay.

She clinched her palms to control her tears and responded, "When the head wins, the heart sinks! But there is a reason why our heart is on the left side, because it is never right!"

Aman looked at her in bemusement and said, "Let's catch up on a cup of coffee this weekend if you are not meeting him. In fact, he can also join us. Who would not want to meet a man like him? A salesman meets his clients through networking, right? Who knows if he is the next one."

"Ok sure. Will ask him and confirm." She finally smiled.

As she was stepping out of the car, Aman said, "I don't know your story. But the heart is never wrong. Heart sinks because of the helplessness to avoid the calamity that's going to strike us and not because of the battle it has lost."

Flashback – First meeting

"I am busy, Leyla. Call you later." Vikrant disconnected the call, without bothering about what Leyla had to say.

It was his usual reply. Leyla could not understand the reason for this sudden change in Vikrant's behaviour which was causing havoc in Leyla's heart and mind. But she trusted him. She wanted to be patient till Vikrant came back and told her the reason himself. He was her mentor first. She had full faith in her mentor. He couldn't go wrong.

Vikrant called back after a couple of hours.

"Good morning, Vikrant! I got up early, got ready, had breakfast and convinced mom to allow me to be out for the whole day and let me enjoy my weekend!" Leyla said in her chirpy voice.

"Good morning, sweetheart. But my apologies, I won't be able meet you today. My boss has kept an urgent meeting on design review as we need to meet the deadline. I have to attend the meeting. But will surely catch up with you in the evening," Vikrant said.

"Ohh Vicky! That's sad, but I understand. But can they call you during your mandatory leaves too?" Leyla didn't want to reveal her disappointment to Vikrant.

"Oh yes darling! Why not? Though it's not allowed and I don't usually access my emails and laptop. I am going there to guide the team, as a consultant to my team," Vikrant clarified.

"Oh ok. But Vicky, I had already confirmed to Mr. Aman Malik, my boss, about our meeting today. He wanted to meet both of us over the weekend, remember?" Leyla asked.

"Ohh well, please apologize to him on my behalf. You should carry on with him. I will join you next time for sure," Vikrant said.

"Okay Vikrant. Love you!"

"Bye."

She was disappointed but consoled herself by thinking that he must be genuinely busy today. Leyla called Aman and decided to meet him for coffee.

She chose a black short dress along with a pearl necklace. She tied her hair into a bun and studded it with a pearl hairpin.

"Hi Leyla. I am waiting outside your house. How long will you take?" Aman called and told Leyla.

"Hi sir, errr Aman. Will be there in two minutes."

"Old habits die hard. See you!"

Aman was stunned looking at Leyla. He had never imagined she could look so beautiful and elegant. Leyla looked so simple in her usual office attire. As she sat in the car, Aman could no longer hold the compliment back and said, "You look gorgeous Leyla! For a second I thought I have come to the wrong address. It took me a moment to realise that it is really you. It is 'The Vikrant magic' I believe".

Leyla blushed and said, "Thanks! That's a sign that you have chosen the right partner." Leyla's tone was a little sarcastic.

Aman pouted his lips, raised his eyebrows, expressed his agreement in embarrassment and quickly changed the topic. "So who would choose the venue for today's meeting?"

"Let us go with your choice. I need a break from my choice today!" She chuckled.

"Okay. Let's go to Select Citywalk in Saket. I need to buy some shirts too. Will buy some if we have time."

"Okay."

"It has been a long time since somebody made me realise that I am a workaholic! Thanks for reminding me. I am going out on a weekend, to have fun, after two years. I usually attend business meetings or go out for drinks with clients who are friends now. Mundane, isn't it?"

"My pleasure sir, sorry, Aman"

Aman dropped the car for valet parking and walked inside the mall with Leyla. They entered The Coffee Bean & Tea Leaf. They settled for a table in the corner, near the glass window and ordered two café macchiatos.

That day they chatted for about half a day without realising the time. They still had so much left to talk about.

Suddenly Aman asked, "Leyla, tell me about your first meeting with Vikrant. Was it awkward to meet him in person? I mean, finally giving face to the voice that you had been listening to, for so long?"

Leyla smiled. She had almost forgotten about the beautiful moments she had spent with Vikrant. Aman's sudden question about the first meeting filled Leyla's heart with happiness and her eyes with a spark as she narrated the story to Aman.

Vikrant was born and brought up in Bangalore and had never visited New Delhi besides the New Delhi airport during transits. Leyla was extremely excited about his arrival, but deep down she feared the first meeting. Her biggest fear was to relate to the voice she had heard all this while with the man whom she was going to see. What if she started searching Avi in him? What if she disliked Vikrant and he got to know that by her expressions? She was both cautious and guilty. Vikrant was super excited though. He did a lot of shopping and planned his wardrobe for each date, unaware of Leyla's apprehensions.

It was 27 November, 8:10 a.m. Dressed in a rose pink, flared georgette top and black leggings, Leyla was anxiously waiting outside the airport when Vikrant called her on the phone.

"Where are you darls? I am outside gate number two."

"I am also near gate number two. Let me walk towards the gate."

"Leyla, get your car outside the parking. I have a lot of luggage to be carried."

"Okay! I will meet you opposite gate number 2. It is White Corolla DLBC 5427."

"Great!"

Leyla drove to gate number two and anxiously looked for Vikrant amidst the crowd. Then a guy in denims and a multi-colour, striped sweater, walked towards her. He was carrying a long black coat and scrolling over a loaded trolley with luggage. His appearance was impressive with a tall and a broad silhouette. Leyla could not relate this man to the voice she had been hearing all this while. It was when he walked closer that he smiled at

Leyla. But she was still nervous to exchange the gesture. Vikrant touched her cheek and whispered, "It's me, darling! That's me. Your Vicky!"

"I couldn't relate with your face, but your touch is so familiar, Vicky. It's so reassuring." Leyla said, but doubted if she really meant it. She hurriedly hugged him and instantly stepped back.

"Unlock the car's boot, darls. Let's move from here before you end up creating a traffic chaos," said Vikrant.

"Sure."

They drove towards the hotel. On the way, Vikrant talked about Delhi roads which were wide and clean, the multi-lane flyovers and the metro. He had never imagined Delhi to be this developed and organised. Leyla was much more comfortable with him now. She told him that he must visit old Delhi to experience the old-world charm with the original, chaotic feel of India.

Leyla parked the car outside the hotel. She helped him in unloading the luggage, but then she thought how can she accompany an unknown man to his hotel room? As Vikrant made a move, she paused in the confusion. He looked back and attempted to read her mind. Gauging her inhibitions, he held her hand tightly and made her feel comfortable. There was something reassuring about Vikrant which made her feel safe. Leyla felt that this deep, silent moment had cleared all her doubts about his intentions. As they entered the lobby, Vikrant noticed the look on Leyla's face, as the house keeping staff looked at her. He murmured in her ears, "You are my only family, Leyla. Let me handle the situation. You are my woman and I will do everything to save your dignity."

Vikrant walked to the reception and said, "There is a room booked by the name of Vikrant Rao, single occupancy. It is under corporate plan for the employees of Carnival Software Inc."

The receptionist said, "Yes sir. Your room number is 309. Please take the first right from the escalators on the third floor." He instructed a staff member to carry the luggage and help Vikrant to locate the room. Vikrant was about to make a move when the receptionist asked, "Does ma'am also have a booking with us?"

Vikrant paused and replied, "No. She is my extended family in Delhi. She facilitated the transit for me. I hope you will be courteous enough to get us some tea and sandwiches in the room till she is here." His was polite but firm. The receptionist felt embarrassed and quickly nodded in agreement.

Leyla entered the room with apprehensions. But as the house keeper left the room, Vikrant held her hand in his and planted a soft kiss on the back of her hand. He said, "I did imagine myself doing this while I was in flight. Since we did not meet in college or on the job or near our residence, it was natural for me to imagine myself holding you and make you feel like the most important woman in the world. Anytime I would have thought of meeting you, this would have happened. Our love story is different Leyla, so should be your first meeting."

Leyla's eyes were moist with emotions. She found Vikrant to be extremely sensitive and understanding. This was the first time Leyla felt like she loved this man. She placed her head on his broad chest and took a deep breath. Leyla couldn't hold her tears back and they rolled out on her cheeks. Vikrant immersed her in his warm embrace. He whispered again, "You are far more beautiful than I had imagined you in my thoughts and from your pictures. You are my angel, Leyla. Will you take care of your devil?"

Leyla softly replied to him, "You are a true human being, Vikrant. Who says you are a devil? You are the most precious gem of my life."

He kissed on her neck and loosened the knot in her hair. Her silky hair fell on her shoulders and her face. He picked up each strand from her face and settled it behind her ears. He looked at her again and said, "I finally get to see you darling! I finally get to touch you, feel you. Your face is so captivating. Your skin soft as velvet. The blush on your face, when you had got nervous at the airport, made you look like a cute little cherry!"

Leyla was mesmerized in his embrace and kept holding him tightly. Vikrant took her face in his hands and pulled it closer to his lips. His deep brown eyes kept staring into hers. Slowly, he pressed his lips against hers. Leyla felt an adrenaline rush throughout her body. Leyla's lips parted and they melted in each other's warmth.

The house keeper knocked on the door, ready with tea with snacks. Leyla was a little embarrassed. She immediately snuggled-out of his embrace and opened the door without looking at Vikrant. As she was directing the housekeeper on where to place the eateries, Vikrant took out a few sheets of paper from his handbag and handed them over to Leyla. She looked surprised and asked him, "What's this Vicky?"

"Well, sometimes, I used to sit in a cafeteria over the weekends and write about you. Just a few random thoughts on paper. Do read it in your free time."

Leyla had her evening tea with him and left for the day. As she reached home, she immediately took the sheets out of her purse and started reading.

"In the distance, too far for any humane eye to see under the raging thickness of concrete woods. A discovery nonetheless leaves me in fascination, how could something so serene, be existing at such a depth, and yet still be surviving without moving an expression of difference, as an act against the disparagement that is so entwined into this modern world. There is very wide wonder as to how she manages to keep herself afloat whilst still being submerged in the quicksand of life's relations. And when I did move close with curiosity, I was taken into an eye-widening astonishment that this person actually springs out, with life bubbling around, with childish and impish expressions surrounding her index. Innocence sprawls from those indented eyes, which in today's world actually exists in the seldom handful, as though she has been given the right to out flood it on to her dear ones. Petal by petal, as I extract one by one to look what is inside, I move with great care and fragility.

"To my delight, I can't help myself to wander, in amazement, through an expanse flushed and populated by all those fantasy creatures, in fairy tales. The disposition of events from her narration could provide an author the source of a 'Definite Inspiration' to apply a bevelling-cut to a 'Character Sketch' of any unanimated entity which needs just about anything to be flowing with variable moods. Take her tears and dry them up to an hardened ash or freeze them below a temperature where any life form would suffocate to death. It still has enough strength to provide a lifetime span when sprinkled over the unincarnateable mummy of Tutankhamen, though when coming to life the mummy's first word would not be "mother" or "father" or anything close to referring a parent or a caretaker in the long vast lost and yet present languages for I know deep inside the word is 'Why' or 'kyu?' for beginners.

"Take the entire number of mentors in this planet, including the various ways nature can teach each of the life form that flourishes on it, and one would still fall short to compare it to the number of questions that arise within her. Some trivial, some natural, some expected, some sarcastic, some relative, some very detached, quite a few mundane and most of them ethereal (surreal). There's no scope for convincing her about the answers that one can give, for not one of you possesses the understanding of her questions, you morons! It takes an immense amount of scope that should be delved in with deepening knowledge equipped with astounding brilliance to blast light into the oblivion, that would beam the dark road to eternity in ever-shining gleam of luminous rays that gleam with defiance extending into infinity beyond the horizon.

"Though I have to etch here that this is just two-thirds of the paraphernalia that should be armed with an extemporaneously insane perspicacity of valorous logic that dauntlessly dawns on all ignorance, and if this doesn't come natural at the very instant whence providing or proposing a solution, then be ready to be sized up with the most insignificant unwanted creatures residing in unrewarded dungeons in her vision. I know you are already whirlpooled there. Her thoughts are extensively characterized by fantastic imagery and incongruous juxtapositions taking me to a great concourse of phantasmagorical shadows that lurk in the light as well as visible in the dark. In every paradigm, her brain never ceases to separate from 'what is discovered' and 'what remains undiscovered' to 'what is already invented' to 'what needs to be invented and which needs to be renovated'.

"A glance into her paradigm and I end up viewing imagery that is more life-sprawling than the Nutcrackers Ballad, or even Alice in her wonderland for that matter. There is no opera that is more sonorous than the musical phantom in her rumination. No such thespian can ever be adorned to amount of directive verves that can nerve in any human. Her sense towards a commitment is so idealistic that the most committed commitment shames itself away for being definable just within a sentence. Her grit towards an aim that she sets to achieve leaves the meanings of determination, dedication and devotion in voidness, for when she summons a force that beckons from her heart, there is no strength that can divert such an honed effort. Her eyes gleam with an accuracy more sure than the imagery analysed by the sensors aboard the USS Tomahawk.

"You are a pure unadulterated slandered morsel of living meat if you think you can pen or type her name down and say there's a great deal about her, for even in this hour of language literature pinnacles, she stands as a bright apex in my vision to be an inspiration to challenge the limits of the most vast literature at the command to describe her. To aggregate the thoughts above, she comes with a complementing condescending heart that denigrates the ones held by angels. The compassion displaced once withered from within her is truly magnanimous, inching every bit of that difficult distance she gives her best to nudge unending support through what little strength she can unravel from within her amidst the suffering that toils this world. She never sets a step back in procuring anything that her heart desires for, a deep rooted shoulder benign every life form she feels for. Her sense of humanistic values and bonds makes me desire the need to dive and drown in their essences.

"The aroma that spontaneously and sporadically emerges from her being is so enthralling that it eventually takes over my senses and helplessly pulls my foot to barge in uninvited and rest in the greatest splendour of what accompaniment this human can provide. She holds the ability to fuel my so sophisticated carnal desires to a savory saccharine that churns more wisdom than the divine ambrosia. Every feeling that I expose livens up in her to the brightest shine as she polishes them with her enchanting touch. She drives a passion so deafeningly flowing towards me that for the Diablo in me she condign as a divine angel in camaraderie, thus making her my eternal pavickyur."

Tears were rolling over her cheeks as she finished reading. What Vikrant had shared with her had touched the bottom of her heart. She felt glad to have met this man in her life. While arranging the sheets, she noticed a small pink slip in-between. It read,

"For if in love you greatly comply and believe
then dear take your hand and touch the breeze
feel the flow in your hearts glow
it's not what nature provides
it's the wish that comes along as I guide
hold me in embrace, my doll
for there's always me to hold even in mutual fall."

She instantly knew that was the answer to all her whys and what her insecurities compelled her to answer. With moist eyes, she messaged Vikrant, "I am thankful to god for having gifted his best soul to me. I love you Vikrant! I love you so much."

Vikrant replied, "You are inducted in me, darling. I am glad you loved it. I am glad you read it. I am happy you feel every emotion that I have for you. I love you too, more than I thought I will."

•

Aman was mesmerized with her love story, but he felt bad when he recalled that the perfect love story was vulnerable right now. There was something that was not going right at present. He somehow felt that Maya was the reason which had soured their relationship. He asked Leyla about Maya's entry in their paradise.

Leyla and Maya met almost after a decade. She recollected how excited Vikrant was about Maya's first interview. And his strong reaction on Maya being selected in the same company as hers.

Vikrant looked at the mirror in his steel-grey shirt and black trousers and wore a black necktie with silver polka dots on it. He looked up at the clock and realised that it was 6:50 a.m. He called the receptionist to check if the breakfast is laid since he wanted to reach before time on the first day in office. He wanted to be ready with the meeting agendas before his team arrived. Vikrant was known for his punctuality, preparedness and detailed knowledge of the processes while Leyla was just the opposite.

He was thinking about how well they complement each other in their strengths and weaknesses when Leyla called him up.

"Good morning, darling, I was just thinking about you." Vikrant said after taking the call.

"Good morning, Vicky! Wanted to wish you luck for the first day in office. I hope you love it here!" Leyla replied in her usual chirpy voice.

"I already love it here, for this has brought me closer to you. Thanks for your wishes, honey. So, what are your plans for today? If you are not preoccupied, why don't you join me for lunch?" asked Vikrant.

"I wish I could, Vikrant. But I just received an e-mail from the HR of JSM Investment bank. I had dropped in my application for the role of business development manager. The interview is scheduled between 10 a.m. to 2 p.m. in Gurgaon. I am not sure if I can join in for lunch, but can surely catch up for dinner. Does that work?"

"But please don't come to meet me empty-handed. I want something."

"What is it that you want, Vikrant?" Leyla was puzzled with this sudden demand.

"An offer letter, dame! I need the offer letter in your hands. It's one of the best companies to work with as far as my knowledge goes."

"Oh Vicky! I love you. You know how to boost my confidence. Muaaaahhhhhh!"

"Muaaaahhhhhh baby! See you in the evening. Today, I am also shifting to the rented accommodation in Defence Colony. I will go to office and shift to the flat in the afternoon.

It is a hectic day, darls. But you better remember that you are inducted in me. All the very best for the very first interview of your life."

"Thanks Vicky. Blush blush. Bye."

•

Vikrant wrapped up the first round of introductory meeting with his team and took a tea break before he began with the training session. He messaged Leyla," Honey, where are you? Done with the interview?"

"Hi sweetheart, done with two rounds and shortlisted. Waiting for the final HR round. Guess what! My childhood friend from school, Maya, is also here for the interview. We were best buddies but had lost touch after school got over. Please pray that she also gets selected. It will be so cool to be with an old friend in a new atmosphere. By the way, how is your day going?"

"Uff! Darls, your playground days are over. It's a corporate where you will work now. No friendships will thrive here. Understand. Anyway, I know my angel won't get it. I will pray for her rejection. My day is cool enough to say the least."

"Vicky!"

"I know. I know. I hear your right inside my head. 'Don't be a devil Vicky!' But darling, I know how vulnerable you are and how ugly corporate world is."

"Why do you always start with suspicion?"

"Because if your suspicion turns out to be wrong, then you always have the scope to trust. But if you start with trust, and you get screwed, then that's it! I know no other way to be perfect, besides this."

"You never cease to impress me!" Leyla exclaimed in excitement.

"And you never cease to be a perfect catalyst of my carnal desires for you. Will eat you up!"

"I am not renewable. How will you get me back again?" Leyla teased Vikrant.

"I will tell you about *how*, tonight @dinner. Getting back to work now. Keep me updated. Muaaah!"

"Okay. Await the dinner. Muaaah!"

Vikrant's trainer, Fernando from Spain, wrapped up the first training session and handed over to Vikrant for additional briefing. Vikrant presented a detailed presentation on client requirements. The deadlines and budget. The discussion was still going on when he received Leyla's message on his phone.

"Vicky! Couldn't clear the final round."

Vikrant immediately excused himself from the meeting and called her back saying, "Hey darling! Don't worry. The screwed-up organization has no idea about what they have lost. Don't worry, we will celebrate their stupidity in some time. Tell me when will you be here pick me up?"

"Very smart! Don't fool me now. I am coming in twenty minutes. Meet me outside your office premises."

"Okay."

Vikrant came back and ended up the discussion within minutes. He enquired if there was an electronic store nearby and rushed out of the office.

Leyla called up Vikrant to locate him. "Where are you Vicky?" she asked.

"Sorry darling. I had to accompany my trainer for some

shopping. I am in MGF mall, opposite my office. This place has got cool restaurants too. Why don't you come here? He is done with his shopping and will leave in five minutes… till you park the car and reach the ground floor, outside Woodland store."

"Okay. See you."

Leyla reached outside Woodland and found Vikrant waiting for her with a gift pack in his hands.

She hugged him tight and asked immediately, "Is it for me? For the rejection? By the way you look irresistible in formals, Vicky! What a stunning shirt!" She blushed.

"Thanks. But no darling, it's not for rejection. It's a bargain for the offer letter that you are going to give to me."

"Oh Vicky! This is unbelievable! How do you know I was lying?" she said with her eyes wide with surprise.

Vikrant hugged her and kissed her left cheek, "Just enjoy. Don't ask how I knew. I know everything about my doll. Congratulations darling! I am so proud of you. Now will you open your gift?"

Leyla quickly unpacked the gift and discovered that it was an Apple iPod! A beautiful silver colour iPod with 8 GB memory. She looked at Vikrant surprisingly. "How do you like it, my big woman?" he asked.

"It's so touching! It is very beautiful, but I don't know if I should take it. It's so costly, Vicky!"

"And so is my woman! Does this not match your taste?"

"But Vicky…" And before she could complete, he kissed her on the lips. "That's the best way to stop a woman from going on and on and on!" They both burst into laughter and walked hand in hand into the Mexican restaurant. Vikrant chose an isolated corner to sit and ordered Enchilada with Lamb Manchaca Filling and Chicken Eldorado with nachos and quesadillas. The decor was the typical, cowboy-Hollywood style, without overdoing it. It was crowded, with a groovy swing to the mood, and flowing with chatter and laughter and the elixirs. Leyla began to share her interview experience with Vikrant. And things about her friend, Maya, "You know Vicky! Her parents were very strict and insensitive. They used to bash her if she did not score good marks or if she would get a negative feedback during parent-teacher meeting. I still remember the marks of thrashing she used to get on her cheeks or arms or thighs. She used to cry the whole day and not eat anything. I have memories of wiping her tears and making her eat my tiffin."

"Really, a strange set of parents she has. So, is she still getting tortured?"

"Yes! That's the part I hated in the entire day. When I asked about it, she went silent and then she tried to cover it up with a fake smile and said, 'They are cool now' I held her hand and told her I am the same Leyla. We might have lost touch, but since we are back together, you can treat me like your old Leyla'."

"That's quite an accommodating gesture, Leyla. "What did she say?"

"Her eyes went moist with tears and she could barely speak after that. I understood everything."

"But the strange part is, she is an adult now. Why can't she revolt?"

"I don't know. We couldn't discuss it anymore. But I told her about you and she was quite happy for me."

"Really? And what all did you tell her, my chirpy lady?"

"That you are so sophisticated, so wise and accommodating. I told her how you asked for six months of my life and changed it forever. That I wouldn't have cracked this interview if you wouldn't have done so much for me."

"Darls, you know I don't like you speaking about me in front of others. How many times did I ask you not to talk about me?"

"But why, Vikrant? I fail to understand the reason. You are my lover now. Why can't I tell people about our relationship?" Leyla snapped.

"Because this world is an ugly place and you are too vulnerable. I want our love to remain in shadows. I can't afford to be vulnerable to save the goodness in me."

"What are you are talking about, Vicky? It makes no sense to me. Maya is just a good old friend. How can she be harmful? In fact, she got very excited after hearing about you, and she wants to meet you."

"Now, why does she want to meet me?" Vikrant said with a grumpy expression.

"I think she wants a mentor too!" She giggled.

"I don't come for free, darls! I take my fees." Vikrant said coldly.

"Really? And what are you charging me?" she said naughtily.

"I will eat you up! By the way, this reminded me that I had to teach you that also!"

"Vicky! By the way, she got selected too. God didn't listen to your prayers, Mr. Devil!"

"Darling, that's what god always does and that's why the devil plots against his play!"

"Vikrant, a devil speaks like god too. How would one

recognise him?"

"Darls, devil only speaks like god to foolish mortals, but acts otherwise. Let's say, god says 'light', devil says 'glamour'. God says 'name', devil says 'fame'. God says 'purpose', devil says 'greed'. God says 'compete with self', devil says 'destroy others'. There is an invisible fine line between the two which is seldom visible. And mortals would not know when that line is crossed and pushes them to the other edge.

Life is an interesting equation!"

"But..."

"Why don't you rather ask me, how would I eat you up and still have you besides me." Vikrant grabbed Leyla in her arms.

"Vicky!"

•

Leyla came home after spending a great evening with Aman. It was a good change for her amidst all this stress of Vikrant's changed behaviour. Was it happening because of Maya? Or was there any other reason? She could not stop thinking about how things had changed. Things that had been perfect, till a few months back.

Aman and Vikrant finally meet

"I will go for a chicken soup," Aman folded the menu and kept it aside.

"Just that?" Vikrant smirked at Aman. "That's why you are so fit. I will order lavishly! What about you Leyla?" Vikrant looked at Leyla.

"Coleslaw salad with some soup." Leyla too decided to keep it light.

Leyla had finally convinced Vikrant to meet Aman. Leyla eagerly waited for the weekend. She wanted to know Aman's opinion about Vikrant. Not that it would change anything about them, but she was keen to know if Aman could correlate Vikrant with the description she had given him.

"So, how is Leyla doing at work?" Vikrant broke the ice.

"She is a promising professional." Aman was delighted to talk about her.

"Good to know that! Although I find her a little vulnerable. She trusts people too easily. I am sure she would get many clients who would promise her good business, but would not live up to the expectations if she counted on them, and make her feel heartbroken later." Vikrant looked at her and smiled.

Leyla did not like it. She did not like it at all! She knew she was still naïve, but Vikrant always respected her and ensured that she was respected by people around her. Why was he criticising her in front of her boss?

She held a fork in her hand and kept poking the table cloth with it in anger, but decided to keep silent.

"I would disagree with you on that. In fact, I find her much sorted. I have been with her to a couple of client meetings. She is graceful and balanced in her approach. Mature for someone of her age and experience, I must say," Aman retorted.

"Thanks Aman. That's very encouraging to hear." Leyla smiled at him

"That's what I wanted to hear. I am glad you found her to be mature; she is my student, you see! This is a result of my mentoring." Vikrant spoke with pride while pouring water in his glass.

Leyla felt awkward and embarrassed with the way he made her feel so inadequate.

"Yes. I am sure. She talks very highly about you, that's why I insisted to meet you." Aman calmly replied.

"Oh! I thought you were also seeking a business investment from my side." Vikrant laughed.

"Well, although we invest in small and medium enterprises corpus, but yes, we can give financial investment tips to friends! Why not?" Aman gracefully replied to Vikrant's odd remarks.

"Friends! Too early to say that, Mr. Malik. We are acquaintances right now. I usually avoid socialising and I take much longer to make friends. Please don't get offended. I am just being frank." Vikrant continued belittling Aman.

"I appreciate your honesty, Vikrant. But I make friends easily. Because I begin with trust. If they break it, I filter them out, because I do believe in giving everyone a fair chance, isn't it?" Aman was calm and settled.

"On the contrary, I begin with suspicion and allow people to win my trust. For how long can you keep hurting yourself because you have a habit of trusting people too easily? There are so many people, with so many ulterior motives!" Vikrant replied.

"Maybe I am lucky. I haven't had many betrayals! To each his own. But why did you agree to meet me without questioning my motive?" Aman smirked in his signature notoriety.

"Because I have a motive to see you." Vikrant bluntly told Aman.

"And that is?" Aman asked him curiously.

"I am anticipating ten million rupees from a project I am currently working on. I need your investment expertise on it," he was quick to reply.

"I believe you work with Carnival Software Inc. How could you earn this big an amount?" Aman grew more curious, rather alert now.

"Well! I am a personal consultant with one big business house. Will give you the details if necessary. My foremost problem is that as per my employment contract, I can't show this income from consultancy since I am not permitted to design any software in my individual capacity, outside of Carnival Software Inc's mandate," Vikrant continued.

Leyla was surprised at Vikrant's revelation. She had absolutely no clue about this. And she was unsure how Aman would take it. She kept looking at Vikrant in complete shock.

"You can't invest with us, till you show this in your books. Our accounts are linked with PAN cards. Anyway, I will introduce you to my CA. He might help you. Once he shows this income in your books, I will personally handle your investments account with us," Aman assured him.

"Oh good. When can I see your CA? I am new in Delhi now, as you know. I don't know many people here. That's why I am dependent on your network." Vikrant told him frankly.

"Well, it's Leyla's network!" Aman smirked at him again.

"Oh yes! You are Leyla's connection for sure." Vikrant finally agreed to give due credit to Leyla for once during that entire meeting. Leyla had had enough. She just wanted them to wrap up their discussion, so that she could leave quickly.

Aman gauged her discomfort and told Vikrant, "Will see you tomorrow, Vikrant. Let's catch up at my house. I will call my CA also. Leyla must be bored with our agendas, she can escape us tomorrow." He laughed and attempted to lighten up the atmosphere for Leyla.

Leyla took a deep breath and called for the cheque. Aman dropped Vikrant to the nearest metro station and offered to drop Leyla to her house since they lived in different directions.

Leyla agreed hesitatingly. She could not gather the courage to ask Aman about Vikrant. He was not even close to what she had described to Aman. In fact, he had been disappointing today.

"Leyla, a man always wants to be ideal in front of her woman," Aman said.

"Yes. But why would you say that?" Leyla was taken aback with his statement.

"I could see that you were neither aware of his agenda, nor about his other source of income. A man prefers not to include his woman to such details, because he wants to stand on the highest moral pedestal in front of you," Aman tried to explain to Leyla.

"Aman, of late, everything has changed. I feel totally unsettled. I don't know what to tell you. Don't know what I would like you to say. I told you that he is almost a perfect human being, but today he appeared flawed and unethical!" Leyla spoke while swallowing her tears which could have betrayed her anytime.

"Nothing has changed, Leyla. You are becoming more aware. We all have imperfections. All of us. Do not burden your people with this 'perfection' syndrome, for they are bound to fail," Aman consoled Leyla.

"But I thought he could never falter." Leyla was still low.

"Why Leyla? He is no god! You are no god. I am not supporting his way of making money. In fact, I will never suggest anyone to do anything against a legal contract. He might invite big trouble for himself. But all I want is that you should not expect godly traits in human beings; you will be always disappointed." Aman continued, "I am curious to know why he told me all this? He does not trust people. Why did he trust me with this confidential information? Maybe what he said is not true, maybe it's something else. I need time and another meeting to figure this out about him," Aman said.

The goof-up!

"Good morning sweetheart! Could you please ask Aman to call his CA in the evening instead this afternoon? I will reach his house around 6 p.m. Please apologise to him on my behalf. I have an urgent meeting with this person, for whom I am designing the software. In fact, you should go and meet him over some coffee. It looks rude to just call and change appointment."

"But Vicky, it is Sunday!"

"Well, since it's my private consultancy, I meet him on Sundays only as I am unavailable on weekdays."

"Okay. Let me call Aman and request him to pick me."

"Done! Bye. Love you!"

"Love you, darling! Bye."

Aman came to pick Leyla at 1 p.m. and learnt about Vikrant's unavailability. In a way, he was relieved and happy. He found Leyla's company positive and refreshing. However, in Vikrant's presence, he could not be carefree.

Aman drove towards hotel Hyatt's coffee shop and dropped the car at valet parking. They walked inside the hotel and Aman opened the door for Leyla to enter. They entered the shop and started looking for a comfortable place to sit. Suddenly, Leyla turned around and clenched Aman's arm tightly, and before he could realise what went wrong, Leyla yelled, "Vikrant!!"

Aman looked in the same direction and said, "Holy crap! What is Maya doing here?"

Leyla looked at Aman in horror and said, "She is with Vikrant."

Maya was totally engrossed in the conversation. She looked up and saw their perturbed faces. She immediately stood up in panic. Vikrant turned around, but his expression did not change at all. He looked at Leyla with cold, unaffected eyes. Leyla held Aman's hand and rushed out of the café. Maya came running and pulled Leyla by her arm.

"Leyla, it's not what you are thinking. Do not act like Avi. Listen to me first, or you will end up thinking that Vikrant cheated on you."

"Okay. I am listening, go on!" Leyla controlled herself to avoid any drama in public. She wanted to get everything sorted, once and for all.

"Listen Leyla, I know it's wrong. I had pressurised him to lie to you about the meeting. Because I got a clean chance to take five lakhs more from my father's safe. And I had to give him the money today only. If in case my dad would have found out and checked with everyone, he would have got to know that I am the culprit. I had to park the money with him." She kept saying in panic, without realising Aman's presence there.

"Five more lakhs!!" yelled Leyla. "But why? Your required only three lakhs, right? That is what you had convinced me for?"

"Leyla, I had a clear chance today. My dad left the locker unlocked and went to the prayer room. At that time, we all were at home, including the maids. Even if he gets to know that five lakhs are missing from his locker, he can't suspect me."

"But why do you need more money, Maya?" she shouted back at her

"Leyla, please think practically. I have to survive in a foreign land. My boyfriend is a student there. I will have no family ties. Just imagine me falling sick. You know how costly medication is over there! What if I meet with an accident there and get hurt?"

"What bullshit are you talking about? You know what, you are not arranging money for contingencies. But you are feeding your greed! Your greed for a better lifestyle. Your greed for comfort, for luxury. And by doing this, you are just not insulting your parent's upbringing, but Shahan's capabilities to keep you comfortable there. Is Shahan aware of what you are doing?"

"No. I haven't told him anything."

"See, there you are! Get lost Maya! Get out of my sight! I don't want to see your face again in my life. In fact, both of you. Tell your bloody mentor, he will burn in hell!" Leyla lashed out at Maya and left with Aman.

She sat in the car, crying desolately. Aman was trying to console her when she received a text message from Vikrant. "I always choose my students. She was never my choice, Leyla, she was yours. Now you understand why I choose people carefully. See what she has done to us? She made me lie to you. She made you find solace with another man. She made us lost and lonely again. For what?? For her selfish interest. That is how this world is, Leyla. You lend them your hand to help and they will suck the last drop of your blood too. I am not going to leave this bitch. I am going to leave her at the cross-roads. Each drop of tear in your eyes made me realise the sin I have committed. What has she made of me within a few months? I am sorry for today, doll. It shall never be repeated. Please forgive your Vicky, just this once."

Leyla kept reading and re-reading the message. Vikrant always used to teach Leyla to read between the lines. For the first time, she was trying to do that with his message. This was not the Vikrant she knew. If he would not be guilty of something, he would never say sorry. He would justify logically; he would give her a proper reason to lie. He would tell her that he never wanted to hurt her. He would argue endlessly, till Leyla would give up and come to terms with him. This was so unlike Vikrant. This message was sent to pacify her and take control of things for the time being. It was damage control, to keep his original mission intact. For the first time, Leyla could clearly see the devil inside Vikrant. The devil who had taken over him. The human being inside him had gone weak.

After reading it several times, she finally replied, "Let me be normal. Give me some time to decide if I can trust you again."

Another shock

Leyla was slowly coming to terms with all that had happened. She decided to take it in her stride and move on. Vikrant was apologetic; he tried to pacify Leyla in every possible way. He disconnected every link with Maya. He gave all his time and attention to Leyla. No matter how well he tried to be back to his old self, their relationship had lost the warmth. Leyla stayed aloof most of the time. Weeks passed by, but Leyla could not move on. Aman told Leyla that he liked Vikrant and she should give him a second chance, but Leyla felt otherwise. She knew that Aman was not comfortable in his presence. Vikrant used to flaunt his knowledge to cover up the embarrassment of the encounter. Leyla could see through the whole drama of ego, of shallowness, of superficial handshakes, artificial smiles and camouflaged appearances.

Leyla looked at her planner and made a few calls. She had a meeting with one of the directors of a prestigious stockbroking firm. She was eyeing on a huge institutional account. Leyla picked her bag and walked towards the lobby when her phone rang. Vikrant had called from the office landline. She picked his phone half-heartedly and said, "Hi Vikrant. Good morning. Reached office?"

"Hi Leyla. This is Kamal. Vikrant's boss. I hope you remember me," Kamal said from the other side.

"Oh! Hi Kamal. I am sorry I took you for Vikrant," Leyla replied in surprise.

"I am shocked, are you not aware that he is hospitalised?" Kamal questioned her in despair.

"*Hospitalized?* What happened to him?" she almost yelled in shock.

"When did you last speak to him?" he enquired.

"We spoke last night, Kamal. He was all right. What happened to him? Please tell me. I am really worried." Leyla was anxious now.

"Leyla, he has not been coming to office since the last twenty-five days. He went on a ten-day leave for his engagement ceremony with you. All of us have been trying to reach him, but his number is switched off. His sister called Abdul last week and informed that he has been diagnosed with tumour. He is getting operated in B'lore City hospital. But after that, we had no news." Kamal spoke without pause.

"What?! Kamal, he is in Delhi only. He is fit and fine. In fact, he has no sister, only a younger brother. He changed his number last month for a better tariff plan. And we never got engaged. In fact, we are facing serious issues in our relationship. I have no idea what you are saying?" she was talking with shock and anger.

"This is strange. Listen Leyla, we are declaring him as an 'absconding' employee." Kamal raised his voice.

"What? But how did you get my number?" Leyla enquired, hastily.

"Luckily, we found your number from a colleague whose phone Vikrant had once used to text you when his phone had conked off." Kamal explained and dismissed the call.

Leyla could not understand what was happening. Did he miss his office to be with Maya? Why had she become an obsession for Vikrant? She thought she would call Vikrant and confront, but she stopped. She had to dig deeper into this. She had to wait for more skeletons to stumble out of the closet. She was now sure that Maya and Vikrant had a story which she was unaware of.

The investigation

"Did you not trust him too soon?" Aman asked Leyla, while sipping his coffee at a café near office.

The last few days had been exceptionally hard for Leyla. Aman made an effort to spend some time with her post office hours. He made Leyla feel sane. She had found a friend in Aman. She sometimes felt a need to ask Aman his reasons to help her in her battle. But she preferred silence over words. She had no scope to invest her thoughts on Aman at this point and jeopardize the bond which they shared.

"I don't know, Aman. I never thought Vikrant would cheat on me for Maya. Maya would never cheat on our friendship!" Leyla said in embarrassment, avoiding looking at Aman in the eye.

"I am actually thinking about something different. It's not an affair that I suspect." Aman pouted while saying this. He was trying to connect the dots.

"I didn't get you Aman." Leyla grew anxious.

"Why did Maya resign the very next day?" Aman was digging into Maya's psyche.

"Obviously! She was ashamed, Aman. What face did she have to come to office after what had happened that day?" Leyla retaliated.

"Maybe what you are saying is right. But could there be a possibility of Vikrant playing a nastier game? They are involved in something fraudulent and Maya resigned to block our access to her? She knew that I was tracking her." Aman was trying to consider all possible reasons for Maya's sudden resignation. Though it was quite predictable, but her appearance in the office next day had no guilt or shame. She rather looked nervous. She was not apologetic, but was in a hurry to finish her mission. He was aware that she wanted to be with Shahan at any cost. That incident must have dented her purpose. Without Vikrant's support, she couldn't have reached her destination. He did not see the grief of defeat in her eyes. She was still unperturbed and focused, despite her fallout with Leyla, her closest friend.

"Yes. I told her last time that you were aware that she is not going for client meetings!" Leyla was still trying to understand Aman's point of view.

"Leyla, can you do me a favour? Could you get Vikrant's investment account here?" Aman said.

"What?" Leyla could not place the direction of the conversation.

"Yes. Tell him that you have target pressures and to save your job, you need his favour. Take a basic cheque of ten thousand rupees." Aman led the way, without revealing his intentions.

"But why?" Leyla exclaimed.

"Give me some time. I will tell you why. By the way, did he graduate from Princeton?" Aman kept the questions going.

"Yes." Leyla was perplexed, but she gave up. She understood that Aman would not divulge his intentions till he would find out something worth mentioning.

"Aman, but why are you helping me so much?" Leyla could not stop herself anymore and asked him.

"Do you really want to know? Are you brave enough to listen?" asked Aman.

"What does that mean? Of course, I am!" Leyla answered back. She was slightly taken aback by Aman's query.

"Are you sure you will not react irrationally or judge me?" Aman posed again.

"You're scaring me off Aman!" Leyla wanted to listen him eagerly now.

"Leyla, I have fallen in love with you. Point blank."

Aman looked right into her eyes. Leyla could not say anything and kept looking at his face. Aman came close to her, still piercing her eyes with his gaze and held her tightly. Leyla was stunned by his intimidation, but could not revolt. He held her face and kissed her lips. Leyla expressed no resistance, as if it was all that she needed at that moment. Why did she not feel offended? She could not understand her own behaviour. Aman's eyes were burning with passion and desire to have her. The desire was so strong that Leyla felt like giving herself away to him. As if he was her true contender. As if he had all the right to have her at that moment. Leyla felt ashamed, embarrassed, yet wanted to stay inside his arms. The thin line between vice and virtue was blurring. She could not hear her inner voice, rather she conveniently chose to ignore the voices in her head.

Leyla had no regret. She did not feel ashamed of anything. At that moment, she dropped her inhibitions and spontaneity flowered. She was withered with the calculations, with all the stress and all the mind games which Vikrant had played with her. She needed spontaneity, and for those few minutes, time ceased for her, her identity did not matter anymore. It didn't matter who she was, who Aman was! She just wanted to flow with time. They were away from the bonds. The bonds that could be named. They didn't bother about the future, the past and about society. The moment was but a flowing expression of her innocence. Leyla had set her mind free and let her heart loose. She felt no burden. The burden of constant calculation. In the last few years, she had seen it all. Love, mind games, molestation, lies, betrayals, impermanence of promises of forever. She was finally understanding that nothing lasts forever. She was finally getting ready to let go. Let go of all the heart-aches from her past, of all the betrayals.

She returned home, opened her diary and penned down a few words.

Who do you think are you in my life?
A friend, a guide or a lover in disguise?
You think I believe in love or in some fairy tale?
I know there is a storm all across and my life is a boat, I need to safely sail…
Life lays a trap here and there at every juncture of choice…
It's difficult not to fall prey to temptations..The only map is your guardian's voice…
I believe in my stars and in my intentions
I wish not to reduce to vices even in contentions…

The path of virtue looks dull and boring...
But the prize I can assure you is a peaceful soul...No
regrets soaring!

She stared at the page and crumbled it. It was the most dishonest poetry she ever wrote. She knew her proximity with Aman would raise many eyebrows. They had kissed in open, they could become the latest corporate scandal. But it didn't matter. People would presume that she was using her boss for her career graph, but it didn't matter. People would call her names, would assassinate her character, but it didn't matter. Avi had attacked her dignity for something she never did. If people would call her names for this, it wouldn't matter. That moment with Aman had liberated her soul, gave her strength that she needed to face what was about to unfold. She had no qualms what so ever.

She picked her pen again and wrote:

He laughs across my face...
His twinkling eyes glance through my necklace...
He runs his fingers through my hair...
Each strand yearns to flow in the air...
What is it that makes me crimson
What is it about him that makes my heart pound and run
That kiss...
& puffing out every time he miss!
His dark hands on my fair skin....
His wandering finger on my chin!
A look in my eyes and knowing what's in my mind...
How does he love me in a form of its kind..

He stands no chance that we both know
Still my heart wants another chance to blow…
Life has played yet another trick…
Our love for the world will be like an eye prick..
Some day I have to bid him good bye…
Because to save two hearts…traditions should not die!

•

She laughed ruthlessly. She was amazed at how life had brought her here. Love was now a game to her. She had grown up wishing to be a one-man woman. Yet life had its own ways. Did she love Aman? No. And she was sure. He was like a drug to her, just like Vikrant. She was now getting aware of her enemy. The enemy was not outside, not her relative who shamelessly molested her, not Avi who failed to reach to her soul, not Vikrant who conveniently changed. The enemy was inside her. Her enemy was her guilt, her low self-esteem, her inability to fight back. Her enemy were her insecurities, her inability to let go, her inability to accept the impermanence of life. No matter what was happening in the outer world, at this moment, her inner world had begun to transform. Despite all the stress she was facing, she had finally begun to see light at the end of the tunnel.

•

Leyla was speaking to her client and explaining him the returns on his investments when she received Aman's message on intercom. "Leyla, come inside, it's urgent"

"I am on a call. Give me some time sir. I am speaking with a potential lead on another phone."

"Leyla, I said it's urgent." Aman disconnected.

Leyla entered and looked at Aman annoyingly. "I was on an urgent call, Aman. What was so important that could not wait for five minutes?"

"Shut up, Leyla and see this report! This is really serious." Aman threw a set of documents across the table.

Leyla hurriedly picked the report and read it. It was Vikrant's CIBIL Report. She read it aloud, "CREDIT INFORMATION BUREAU INDIA LIMITED."

"Yes Leyla. Vikrant's CIBIL report. I am sure that you know about CIBIL but in case you don't know, CIBIL collects and maintains record of an individual's payments pertaining to loans and credit cards. These records are submitted to CIBIL by member banks and credit institutions, on a monthly basis. "

"I don't know what CIBIL score of 550 CIBIL means." She was shivering with fear.

"It means overusing credit cards, lackadaisical with payment of bills and EMI and frequent enquiries for loans, he has done it all. He has an unpaid personal loan of five lakhs, settled credit cards and various outstanding bills are still hovering over his head. A home loan written off in his name is worth forty-five lakhs. And the various loan enquiries which he made recently show that he is still credit hungry."

"Holy crap! But are you sure that it's Vikrant's CIBIL report only? This could be any other Vikrant too!"

"You remember I had asked you to open his investment account with us last month?"

"Yes. I know you told me."

"I got hold of his PAN number from our records and initiated enquiry for his CIBIL score through my friend in a 'retail assets' division of a bank."

"Is he a fraud?"

"According to the bank, *yes!* And this explains why he was encouraging Maya in her unethical ways."

"But Aman, after that incident I had asked Vikrant to give her money back and not stay in touch with her if he wants me back and he did that."

"How are you so sure? You still trust his words?"

"Yes. No. I mean I am sure because Maya texted me the very next evening. See this." She searched Maya's SMS and handed over her phone to Aman.

Aman read the message aloud, "Hi Leyla. I know you hate me after that day, but at least don't punish Vikrant for my deeds. He really loves you and handed over the money back to me. He apologised to me for not being able to help me further. I never asked him the reason and he never explained, but we all know why he did this. Get back to him, Leyla. He is a gem of a person and a genuine human being. Love you, Maya."

Aman was trying to comprehend the message and pacifying Leyla when her phone rang again. It was from Vikrant's land line, again. She knew that it was Kamal again.

"Leyla, we are blacklisting Vikrant on the grounds of leaking extremely confidential information of the project which was yet to be completed. I called you because we suspect that he has sold our project to the competitors." Kamal spoke sternly.

"Kamal, I can't understand a thing. Are you sure he sold-off the company's project?" Leyla was shattered by all that was happening around her.

"No. But the blue print of our project has been leaked. We were trying to figure out how this could be possible. Only four of us had access to the blue print. The other three confidantes are regularly coming to office. It is only Vikrant who has suddenly disappeared. And the lie about getting hospitalised is pointing towards a different story altogether," Kamal explained. Leyla walked out towards the reception to talk.

"Could you give me his new number?" Kamal asked.

"875489789," Leyla hurriedly shared the number with him.

"Thanks Leyla. I know it's hard for you to face this. But consider yourself lucky that you got to know about him sooner than later. And yes, our HR has verified his degree and credentials with Princeton University. He was definitely among the brightest students of the batch, but dropped out in the final semester for reasons unknown. He was never awarded the degree. Therefore, the degree which he shows, is a first-class copy, but not genuine."

"Kamal, let me know if I could be of any more help. Take care."

She disconnected the call and stood at the reception with a blank face. She could not believe that all of this which was happening was for real, and not an illusion. Her colleagues passed by. Some of them gathered around her to see if she was fine. She looked at them and bursted into tears. Aman rushed towards her and asked in dismay, "What happened Leyla? What's wrong?" And she crashed into his arms. She was inconsolable and requested him to take her out of office. He excused the team and rushed out of office with her. He took her to a café nearby and asked her about what had happened. She told him about Kamal's call.

Leyla was shaken up and took deep breaths to keep panic in control. She was clinching her palms and rubbing her neck to regain control. Aman offered her a glass of water and asked her to calm down. "Leyla, please don't mention anything to Vikrant now. Do not mention anything. I have already initiated a background check in his university in Princeton this morning, after I was hinted of a bad CIBIL by my friend. I must get some news in a week's time." Leyla nodded in agreement.

The entire day was filled with extreme stress and anxiety. She could not focus on anything. She had frequent cramps in her stomach and a splitting headache. She had lost both her appetite and sleep. Her parents also noticed her restlessness and asked her twice, but she kept silent. They were getting worried about her, but her dismissiveness kept them at bay.

Aman called her at night and said, "Do you know why he left the US?"

"Why?" Leyla asked him while preparing herself for another bad news.

"Because he made a so-called sister there. She was of American origin, daughter of a divorced couple staying with her mother. He intruded her house and after winning their trust, conned both of them of their bank balance. He knew that strict American laws will screw his life if the ladies took any action. So, he didn't wait for his course to complete and came back to India before they could realise they had been cheated by him. "

"And how do you know about it?"

"Because after a few days of his absence, both the ladies reported the incident to the police and went to the university campus, but the entire effort went in vain. Nobody knew about him and they had no proof that he had cheated them."

Leyla felt an extreme pain in her chest, as if she just got stabbed with a sharp knife.

Next morning, she somehow managed to come to the office and went straight inside Aman's cabin. She stared at Aman's face blankly and waited for him to tell her the next steps.

He instructed her to call Maya and warn her about Vikrant. Leyla called her and said, "Maya, we have just got to know from reliable sources that Vikrant is a fraud. Please don't give him any money and try and get your money back from him."

"Leyla...." Maya's voice was shaking with fear and panic. "Can I meet you right now? It's really urgent."

"Ok. We are coming to pick you up." Leyla understood the urgency and prepared herself for further revelations.

They picked up Maya. They were shocked to see her pale and shabby.

"What's wrong Maya?" asked Leyla hurriedly.

"How can you say he is a fraud?" Maya asked her. She was nervous.

Leyla took out the CIBIL report from her bag and handed it over to Maya. She explained to her about the chain of events which had taken place in the last few days. She also showed her the message that Vikrant had sent her against Maya.

"Maya, but why you are so scared? You already took your money back and messaged me too. Didn't you?" asked Leyla.

"Shit! No Leyla. He asked me to send you that message to make you believe that we are not in touch anymore. That Vikrant is not helping me anymore and his only concern is saving your relationship with him."

"What? And you agreed to lie to me? How could you Maya? Lying to your childhood friend for someone you met only a few months ago?" Leyla broke into tears of despair and hurt.

"Leyla! I thought this could save your relationship and could help me reach a step closer to Shahan. I told that lie for everyone's sake, Leyla, trust me." Maya tried to explain.

"And now? Who's good has your lie served Maya? None, right? We all are screwed."

"Leyla, without wasting any more time, let's visit Vikrant's place. I am sure we will be able to catch him."

"No no no. I am sure Kamal must have called him up by now on his new number and he would have been alerted. Since only Leyla can provide Vikrant's new number to Kamal, I am sure he is smart enough to understand that Leyla knows the truth by now." Aman interrupted, "Leyla, did Vikrant call you after you spoke to Kamal?"

"No! Hell no. I never realised amid this stress. We have not spoken in the last forty-eight hours," Leyla exclaimed.

"What should we do now?" Maya asked.

"Maya is still in his good books. After all, he has taken five lakhs from her and he might be planning to extract more from her. Maya, please call him and ask him to meet you at Cafe Blue. His greed will be your bait. Tell him that you have more money to give him."

"Guys! I can't tell him that, because he knows it's impossible to get even a single penny from my home now. It's not just five lakhs. I am afraid to say this, but I have given him jewellery worth thirty-five lakhs. My mom's solitaire rings and a set of single line diamond bangles and a diamond set. And hard cash of fifty lakhs." Maya spoke in shame and disgust.

"What? Are you kidding us, Maya?" Aman snapped at Maya in astonishment.

Leyla's jaw dropped. "Your parents still have no idea?"

"They think our house has been robbed. An FIR has already been lodged and my parents are doubting me as well because they caught hold of my TEOFL certificate. Though I have told them that I took it to test my abilities, they assume that I had plans to elope with someone. And I might have given it to my boyfriend. Since they have no proof, they are unable to take any action against me. But my plight in my own house is pitiable. Nobody trusts me. They keep their almirahs locked in my presence."

"Maya, no matter how much I hate you right now, I suggest not to waste a single minute and call Vikrant. Let's invite him for some coffee." Aman said and went aside at a distance to make some calls.

As instructed, Vikrant was invited after an hour. As he appeared, he saw Leyla and Aman in front of him. Suddenly, Leyla realised that four men with a strong build, looking like bouncers were also there. They were taking instructions from Aman. She understood Aman had planned the defence as well as prepared for an anticipated attack on Vikrant. Vikrant looked at them. He was still calm and composed. He smirked at Aman. "You guys are so scared of me that you need these rented guards to protect yourself."

Aman was baffled. He yelled at him. "You have been fooling these innocent girls. But I am too seasoned for your games, Mr. Rao."

Vikrant laughed out aloud, and suddenly, a chauffeur-driven Merc S class stopped in front of him. He jumped inside the car immediately and vanished. Before any of them could understand what had happened, Leyla received his call. She picked it up and even before she could say hello, he spoke at the other end, "Dame, so today you are ready to get your mentor bashed by these rented bastards! You forgot all that we shared, the distance we travelled. You forgot everything, darling. You came with these numbskulls to get hold of me! I always told you that you are vulnerable. Today you proved it, darling. How easily you saw me getting into danger and how conveniently did you push me into it! Have you ever loved anybody? Have you ever understood what love is? I am ashamed of loving you. They will never get hold of me. But I still love you, my woman. I am leaving for Bangalore today evening, never to come back to Delhi. Would love to see you at my apartment! Make sure you come alone, otherwise you know I am LE DIABLE!"

The phone got disconnected. Leyla stood with a blank expression on her face. The pace of events happening in her life was way ahead than her understanding. She felt defeated, but comfortable. She felt as if her inner strength had created a protective layer around her. She felt nothing at the moment. No emotions, no pain. Aman and Maya repeatedly asked her about Vikrant's call, but she could utter nothing. The question kept ringing in her ears, "Have you ever loved anybody?" The smirking faces of Avi, Vikrant, Aman, her family, all that came in front of her. As if they all were asking her the same question. "Have you ever loved us? Have you ever loved anyone? Whom do you love, Leyla? Who are you living for? Are you only living for you? Have you ever been completely devoted to anyone? Good, bad, and ugly, whatever we are! Did you love us unconditionally?"

Molestation was a poison that was flowing in her blood. It needed an antidote. Avi, Vikrant and Aman were all antidotes. True love had never occurred in her life. Did she ever love anyone? How can one fall in love when one hasn't loved oneself enough? She was hollow. She wouldn't have forgiven herself for allowing herself to be a victim of someone's lust. She didn't love herself enough. How could she give away something which she never had? She wanted to embark on the spiritual path, on the path of self-discovery. It was her first lesson in that direction. To love others, you must first love yourself.

To forgive others, you must first forgive yourself. To reach god, you must first reach yourself. God can wait!

Leyla smiled in oblivion. She was in a state of joy. A veil had been lifted. Her failed relationships now made sense to her. She had been a prisoner of her grief so far. For the first time, she was free of her grief. She was liberated. Traumas are treated by shocks. Distrust had to be treated with distrust. It was the therapy of the universe.

Leyla preferred to explain none of this. She took a taxi and rushed to Vikrant's apartment, leaving everyone behind. As she entered the apartment, she found Vikrant waiting for her. He was sitting on his favourite wooden armchair. The apartment was a complete mess with countless cartons lying everywhere in the hall. The room was stinking as if it had not been exposed to sunlight for a long time. She could see rats running around and nibbling the cartons. There were spider webs all over the walls. She looked at Vikrant in complete shock, "Do you live here Vikrant, in this hell?"

"Oh no darling. I only keep my things here. I have been staying in exclusive 5-star hotel rooms, sweetheart!"

"Since?"

"Since few months."

"With Maya's money?"

"Is it truly Maya's money? Has she earned it? Did she get it rightfully?"

"Have you got it rightfully? Have you earned it?"

"Ohh darling! You are too innocent and vulnerable!"

"Maybe I am, Vikrant. But I am not a fraud. I am not a cheat."

"You know nothing, honey. It's not even the tip of the iceberg that you know about." He cracked into a loud and eerie laughter.

"What have you done with her money?"

"Ohhh honey, stop saying that now. It's not her money. How many times do I have to tell you that? People earn money. I make money. A lot of money indeed." He laughed again, in the same strange voice.

"Look at this honey! You really think I didn't love you? See this." Vikrant opened a few cartons.

Leyla was stunned to look at beautiful, heavy embroidered saris and dresses. The other carton had beautiful footwear, stylish hats and expensive handbags. Vikrant opened another suitcase and took out a bridal dress in red and green colour. It was studded with beautiful embellishments which gave it a premium feel.

"This is for you, Leyla! Countless dresses for our honeymoon. Stylish hats and matching jewellery. I wanted to pamper you. I wanted to see you as a queen. My queen! You have never seen love, Leyla. You have never felt madness. You have never felt true happiness, Leyla. I wanted you to be the happiest wife. The most stylish and proud wife. You know I hired that Merc to show you your own city in style. But you never understood me, Leyla. You could never see that I was doing everything for you. You just drifted away. You confided in another man. You thought I am mean? How could you even say that, Leyla? It was all for you!"

"Vikrant, did I ever tell you that I wanted to be a queen by robbing another king's palace? Did I ever tell you that?"

"Leyla! Look at history. Countries were colonized and exploited. Precious things were looted. Kingdoms were won through battles or by dirty tricks. Leyla, history has taught me. Maya had to rob her house to reach Shahan. And how did her father earn this money? He robbed the government. He did not pay taxes. Maya did it for her love and I did it for you. Who is a criminal? If I am, then she is a criminal too. Why are you standing by her side and not with your man?"

"Vikrant! Why did you allow the devil inside you to take over?" Leyla helplessly broke into tears.

"Because my angel lost trust on me. She left me! I would have returned every penny to Maya with huge returns. I invested half of her money in safe haven to secure her future and with the other half, I bargained your happiness. But you gave me no time to explain and came with bouncers instead!"

"I don't trust you, Vikrant. Not anymore. If it's true, then why are you running away? Why didn't you answer any of us? Why didn't you return her money before leaving?"

"I have been declared a criminal. So at least now I should justify the title. But you will always miss a soulmate in this lifetime. We are inseparable, darling. I am the devil and you are my angel. No matter where you will be, or whoever you marry. Whether you become a mother or a grandmother at whatever age and stage of life you will be, you will be incomplete without me. You will lead a lonely life, Leyla. A life to show this world that you won. But you will lose every day. I am the one you chose. Whether I am the vice or the cunning devil, I am yours. And you are leaving me to prove this world your righteousness. You will lose, Leyla. A stupid bargain you are making! You are my soul mate…" His voice started to fade away. He left the room. The apartment. And the road. He was walking away. In few hours, he would leave the city and Leyla's life. Leyla could have stopped him. She could have called Aman and allowed him to tackle this his way. The money could have been recovered, if not fully, then partially. But she did not feel like stopping him. He had always warned that he never came for free. He took his fees. He did exactly what he had said. He was never meant to be. How could she be so wrong! Leyla thought to herself. It didn't matter now. Did she help him elope? Did she help him succeeding in his plans? She had no answer. Neither did she want one. She was ready to throw away all the doubts and questions he had left her with. Leyla was ready to embark on her new journey.

She would never be the same again. Neither did she intend to. Life was a long road home. She was ready for her new challenge, before she found her final abode! She had got her second lesson. Life tests all. It will knead our patience. It will make things intolerable. Each one of us will hit the rock bottom. Some will bounce back. Rest will succumb to the fall. Things will not be easy for those who get up. Roads ahead will get steeper and tough to trudge. Destiny will look farther. Principles will be left behind. Opinions will change. Experiences will astonish the mind. Yet the strongest will reach there. She had heard, "View is beautiful from the top." She knew that her ultimate lover was waiting on the top, on the pinnacle. But before she could merge with her lover, she had to cross many miles, had to climb steep hills, had to fathom deep oceans, had to meet the demons so that finally, she could rest in peace in the embrace of her true love. Till then, love could wait...

She lived a few lives within a life....
Behind her, few stories rest in peace...
She, but stayed nowhere ... she cared for none to please...!
With each story that lay dead beneath the steps she took ahead....
There were also laying some portion of her skin she had to shed...
She kept wondering... why each story had to die...
Was she the living phoenix born out of ashes ... now ready to fly?